Everything is True

but not necessarily factual

Everything is True

but not necessarily factual

Stories

Welton Rotz

TC Publishing
San Francisco

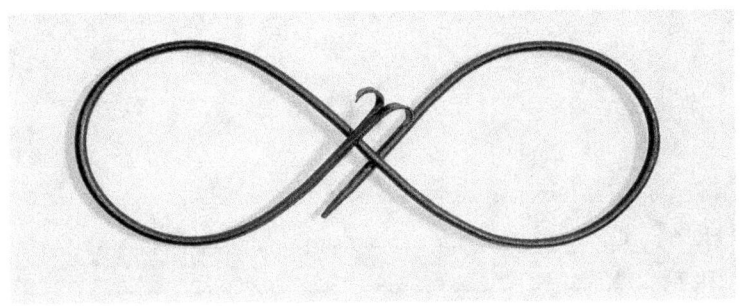

To Barbara, my wife and life companion,
for her encouragement and understanding on my journey
as a sculptor and as an author

CONTENTS

INTRODUCTION

Everything is true, but not necessarily factual.

Truth can contain facts, but also beliefs and make beliefs.
I experienced or was involved in every story in this book.

Memories of my childhood are vivid.
Some have been added to.
However, they are still true.
In the story "Why" I did toss the bottle overboard with a note and did receive an answer a few years later. This story is what might have happened.

My cousin David, my farming partner, had difficulty finding a wife. When he did, he was saddened by his marriage. He died at fifty-six with a broken heart. The story "Visitor" is my alternate life story for him.

For over fifty years my spiritual explorations and development have been a symbiotic part of my artistic creations.

In writing these stories my source of inspiration, my creative higher self, has been a constant partner, just as it was in my sculpting.

THE STOOP

An old man was just sitting there on a block of concrete in the middle of the prairie, his feet on the first step, and his arms resting on his knees. As we drove past he glanced up and I gave a wave. We are on our way to pick up a tractor left in the field after plowing. He responded with a small hand gesture, a two-finger hand wave. That's the way it's done out here.

"Did you see that?" I asked my cousin David, "Just sitting there." We're working together during summer break.

"Yeah, that's the old Baldwin place," he said.

"Why is he just sitting there?"

"I don't know for sure," David said. "I don't come by here much, but often he's out there just sitting."

"But why?"

"There are a lot of stories," David answered. "Some say after his kids grew up and left, his wife ran off. When she didn't return, he burned the house down to get rid of all of the memories. But I don't believe that. Sounds like mean spirited gossip to me."

"Yeah, it does." I looked back. "What else?"

"More likely, one night a tornado destroyed the house. They say, the next day the neighbors found him with a gash in his head laying under a mattress in the front yard." David glanced out at the fields. "They found his wife, what was left of her, a few days later in the middle of a field, about half a mile away."

"That's pretty sad," I said. "It all seems sad."

"Yep," David continued, "I think he's living with his daughter and her family in town. He sleeps in the storm cellar, which must be pretty uncomfortable."

"What's a storm cellar?" I asked.

"Just a hole dug under a house," David answered. "Not like a basement with four walls and the floor. Sometimes people have a shelf with Mason jars filled with canned fruit and vegetables." He shook his head. "But nowadays who has time for canning?"

"Maybe he feels safer there," I said.

"Yeah, I don't think his house had a storm cellar," David said. "His son-in-law and grandson are farming the place now."

Later in the day, I drove the pickup home. The old man and his rust-red pickup were gone.

*　*　*

It is almost harvest time and everyone is waiting. The machinery, the combines and trucks, are serviced and ready to go. The bins used for storing seed wheat are cleaned and ready. An extra hired hand is put on for harvest, and he's kept busy hoeing weeds between the trees in the wind break. I have the time, so after breakfast, I head out past the old Baldwin place. The old man is not there. The field around the place has been planted. I hesitate to roll over the crop, but I see car tracks through the wheat, so I drive up to the stoop.

I get out and the wind catches the truck door and slams it shut. I have heard it said about western Kansas; "It ain't nothing to see a brick rolling down the road in the wind." I have never seen it myself, so I can't verify the truth of this. The only sound is the sssssssinging of the wheat in the wind, and the birds darting and swooping around catching grasshoppers.

I go up to the block of concrete, two steps tall, about three feet wide, and maybe four feet deep. I stand on top. This was the portal, the gateway to the house, to the home. A passageway, through the front door, from the outer world to the inner world. Now there is no house. Behind the block, peeking through the underbrush, are some weathered wooden floor boards. Most of the weeds are bright yellow sunflowers or vines of wild gourds, no doubt planted years ago by a bird's droppings. I wonder if a coyote has made her den in the underbrush. Beyond the tangle of boards and vines is a Cottonwood tree, it also having been planted by nature, since the tornado. The Native Americans of the Great Plains hold the Cottonwood tree in great respect. The heart-shaped leaves constantly quaking, and rustling in the wind, speak of life itself. They believe the tree is a gateway to the afterlife.

The concrete stoop seems grossly out of place here on the prairie, with the wheat planted right up next to the block. Its gray solidness stands out in sharp contrast to the moving, singing, undulating green and amber wheat. As I stand on the top, I begin to feel uneasy. My feet tingle, and now my ankles, calves, and knees feel weak. All around me is movement; the wind blowing through wheat, the Cottonwood leaves shaking, the birds swooping and even my shirt flapping in the wind. I feel nauseous. I feel like the concrete block is moving. No! It is the only thing that did not move in the tornado.

I sit down, my feet on the first step. My arms resting on my knees. This is solid like stone. I have heard of mystical magical stones, in Ireland and Scotland, that are gateways to another dimension. The history of these stones goes way back to the timelessness of legend and fairytales. But I have never heard of a block of concrete with these powers.

I begin to relax. I close my eyes and feel the warm sun. I listen to the sound of the wind in the wheat fields, a sound like no other in the world.

I hear children laughing, and footsteps running on a wooden floor. A door opens behind me, a woman is standing next to me, I feel her presence, I feel her warmth. I feel her hand on my shoulder and neck, the back of her hand grazing my cheek. She says, "Supper is ready." I look up at her, but I cannot see her, the sun is in my eyes.

The wind has been blowing my shirt collar, it's been caressing my shoulder and cheek.

A tightness squeezes around my heart, a quaking and rustling. The beginning of a sob is building in my throat.

"I miss you, oh God, I miss you so much," comes out with the sob. I bury my face in my hands. My body shakes.

The sound of the wind in the wheat has changed. The sound of the almost ripe wheat was a gentle sssssssss, Now the dry, brittle, ripe heads of wheat give a harsher sound, more like shouuuuuu. The wind seems to have died down a little, its job of helping the grain to ripen is now finished. The smell of ripened wheat fills the air; earthy, and full of life. We will start cutting tomorrow. What has just happened sinks in. I walk to the truck to head for home.

I look and see a car coming up the road, a young woman is riding with her arm out the window. She sees me, smiles, and waves. I return her greeting, raise my hand with a two-finger wave. That's the way it's done out here.

MIKEY

"Mikey you naughty, naughty boy," scolded my grandmother.

It was all I could do to keep from laughing. Breakfast at my paternal grandparents was predictable. We had eggs scrambled or fried. Bacon or ham, and cold cereal if we wanted. After breakfast, my grandmother cleared the table and granddad (never grandpa) served everyone a large slice of melon.

My grandmother was large, very large. She had an ample bosom. When my dad was a baby, she served as a wet nurse for the neighbor woman who did not have enough milk for her own newborn.

When she had finished clearing, grandmother opened Mikey's cage door. We were all eating our fruit when she returned to the table. Grandmother placed a bite of fruit between her lips. Mikey flew in and landed on the large expanse of flesh below grandmother's chin and began to eat the fruit. Meanwhile, Grandad came to the table with his reading glasses, the Bible, and a booklet of daily devotions. We were eating our fruit, grandmother was feeding the bird, Grandad was reading the Bible and Mikey...did what birds do. He deposited a tiny black and white dot of poop on the top of the large breast he was standing on.

Grandmother picked up her napkin and began wiping and scolding.

"Mikey, you naughty, naughty boy."

Grandad, lowered today's devotion booklet, looked out over the top of his reading glasses, and scowled at his wife.

"Verna, please," he said, "I'm reading the Bible."

For the last 70 years, every time I hear the Bible read, I hear a voice in the background, "Mikey, you naughty, naughty boy," and I try to keep from laughing.

WHY

In 1953, age 13, I was returning from Europe to New York City on a Holland American Lines passenger/freighter ship. One day out of NYC I put a note with my grandparent's address in Kansas in an aspirin bottle and tossed it overboard. About three years later I received a letter from Normandy, France sent by a sixteen-year-old girl whose fisherman father had found the bottle. She wrote in French, double spaced, with someone else's hand filling in the English translation. We corresponded a few times, me with an awkward teenager's fantasy of having a French girlfriend. Her last letter was very short; "My older brother in the French military, was killed in North Africa." I never heard from her again. I have imagined the grief her family must have had, to have raised a baby during WWII only to have him killed in yet another war. Maybe, her parents stopped the correspondence, because they sensed the potential loss of what was now their only child, to a foreigner.

If only …

I'm standing in the doorway to my room. Across the room is an open window and beyond the beach. The sand and surf and sky stretching away to infinity. It was just a week ago that I was standing in the security line at San Francisco International Airport wondering why I was there.

Am I too old to travel by myself all the way to Paris and then on to the Normandy coast?

The only advantage to being 75 is not having to take off my shoes when passing through security. I was concerned that I might miss my flight; the traffic was so bad the taxi ride took forever. San Francisco is not fun anymore. Too expensive and too crowded. It's not good to be nervous in the security line. I am. However, I am on my way to meet Jacqueline, now the owner of an inn in Normandy, after 60 years. I had reason to be nervous.

I had been sorting through all the stuff that is collected over a lifetime, throwing away the dregs of the past, making room to move from a large house to a small apartment. And there it was, the last letter Jacqueline had written, folded in the bottom of the little wooden chest that holds my keepsakes. I had looked in this chest fifty or a hundred times over the years, and now there it was under the rattlesnake's rattle, under my dad's pocket watch, and under all the other treasures I have collected. Jacqueline's invitation came very soon after my letter of inquiry to her.

The porter brings my rolling luggage to the room, and says I am to meet Jacqueline on the stone terrace. I approach the terrace with some nervousness, but also excitement. There, sitting on a curved, wrought iron chair with her back to me is an old woman, a carved walking stick beside her. Her body is very round, slopping shoulders, hips filling the chair. Was this Jacqueline? Was this the teenage French girl I had dreamed of so many years ago? She turns and smiles with delight and a touch of mirth.

"Come, have a cup of English tea," she says laughing. "Their only decent contribution to world cuisine." Her English is very good.

Jacqueline stands and gives me a little kiss on both cheeks in the French way of greeting. As we embrace, her warmth rushes into my body. We sit and cautiously start to talk. She is not very forthcoming when I ask about herself. I begin with my two marriages, my daughter who has moved away out of state, making visiting difficult, my work, and—

"Enough of this old stuff." Jacqueline jumps up. "Let's go for a walk NOW before the sun sets."

"I need to return to my room to get my cane," I say, seeing her use her walking stick.

On the beach, the sounds of the surf and the sea birds, the smells of the sea and seaweed fill my senses. The afternoon light fades into evening, entwining the whole moment. On the way back, we hold hands. Dinner goes well, the conversation staying in the present; her beloved cactus collection, the vegetables grown in her garden only a few feet away, and the merits of the local wine.

There are periods of silence, but it is okay with each of us. After one of the silences, Jacqueline mentions that her bedroom is just across the hall from mine, on the back of the inn, where she can have the morning sun. She reaches out and touches my hand and very casually invites me to spend the night with her. I became very excited with the thought of sleeping with her! I feel like a sixteen-year-old again.

I am used to a queen-sized bed. Jacqueline's bed is a small European double. We spend considerable effort trying to get comfortable. Jacqueline has the body of a plump matronly woman, but then I am no Greek god myself. We fall asleep, or at least she does. Her snoring keeps me awake. Again, I'm asking, "Why?" The morning sun awakens me, guess I slept more than I thought. As I'm stretching out the kinks, Jacqueline comes in with a bed tray loaded with coffee in cereal sized bowls, and croissants and butter and jam. We have a great breakfast, then playfully make love which includes playing with the flakey croissant crumbs on each other's bodies.

After about an hour, Jacqueline rolls out of bed, and says, "Get dressed because today we are going for a long walk on the beach. The tide is out so the sand is firm. Bring your cane, I can tell you I have a bad knee. I'll bring my walking stick because my hip is acting up."

We walk along, much of the time in silence. The beach sand is firm enough to make walking easy.

"Okay, here is my story." Jacqueline stops. "My father wanted me to marry a fisherman." She looks out to the ocean. "But I held onto my fantasy of my exotic foreigner from the sea; his foretelling by your message in the bottle. I loved my father, but did not want to marry a fisherman. I went to work at the inn, doing duty in every capacity, and at last in the kitchen. The owner and chef liked me and taught me to cook. As he aged I took over much of the running of the inn."

She continues, "One day, as I walked on the beach, I came upon a man crouched over on his knees, sobbing. I held him as he cried. He was English. His father had been killed in the war on one of the beaches in France, but his body was never found. Jonathan, that was his name, had come here to try to find some resolution. He stayed at the inn, we fell in love, he bought the inn, we married and had a daughter. She pretty much runs the inn now...her daughter is away at school. With my hip, I'm slow and the kitchen is small, so, after Jonathan died a few years ago, I just...."

Jacqueline looks out over the ocean. "Enough of the past!" She kicks off her shoes and runs into the surf, shrieking like a little kid. "Come join me."

But I do not want to get wet.

"I'm made of the sea," she shouts.

When she returns, I ask her if she had said "made of the sea," as in constructed of the sea, or "maid (as in young woman) of the sea?" Jacqueline thinks for a moment. Laughing and shaking water from her skirt says, "Both. When I was young, I sometimes heard my parents making love in their room. My father often came home wet from fishing in the sea, and sometimes did not dry himself completely. I imagined some drops of sea water mixed with his spunk when I was conceived. I love the sea."

Jacqueline stops and becomes very serious.

"I have to tell you something. I walk every day on the beach at the water's edge. Sometimes I feel like I dissolve, I can't tell my nose from my toes. But I don't disappear. I become even more real, more present, I'm a part of the whole. I become the sand, the sky, and the sea. Sometimes I think I see angels. It is very frightening, but at the same time very exciting!" She hesitates, looking down the beach, she continues,

"A few years ago, I asked the local priest about my experience. He was kind enough, but dismissed me as being the crazy old woman who walks the beach every day. Have you ever had an experience like this?"

"Yes," I reply, "also by the sea. I was on a bluff overlooking the Pacific just north of San Francisco. Everything I saw was shades of blue: sky-blue, blue-gray ocean, and blue-beige sand. I kept getting bigger and bigger until I no longer fit in my body. I became one with the whole scene, not even the separate parts. I was it all. It changed my life. I began to study spiritual teachings, trying to find what it all meant. I found that some followers spend a lifetime trying to manifest this moment of being at one with the Divine."

Jacqueline reaches up and touches my face. Her fingers remain. I can feel love in her touch. I put my arm around her and pull her close. We kiss. Our embrace relaxes, we pull apart, looking at each other.

"How does a person use this special place in daily life?" she asks.

"Artists," I say, "do their creativity in this place, even though they may not know it. They say: 'My muse told me, or an inner being moved my hand, or the stone talked to me as to where and how to carve.'"

Jacqueline nods with understanding.

"We are both truly blessed," I say, "to have had this powerful experience. I have also found in my studies that when one is in this special place, that is when co-creation can take place. When we humans are co-creating together with the Divine, anything and everything is possible." I look down, and lifting my head, glance out to sea. "It is important to keep the memory of this special experience and this place present in one's mind as we go about our daily life. It may not seem earth shaking, but we are creating all the time."

Jacqueline steps close to me. I think she is going to embrace me, but instead she holds my arms with her hands, just above the elbows. The leather thong of her walking stick looped over her wrist. Looking up at me, she says;

"You have given me a great gift, the gift of understanding what this special place truly is. I'm very grateful."

She gives me a little hug, turns, and still holding one arm starts to walk.

"I'm going to tell you something I have never told anyone. I have thought about you, or more exactly who you might be, off and on for many years. I was in a fantasy world: you came to me from the sea, the exotic foreigner." She pauses, then continues. "Maybe it was a good thing that my father forbid me to continue writing to you. I don't know if you could have lived up to my fantasies."

She stops, looks up at me. "A few weeks ago, maybe a month, I was walking and I was in that special place, and instead of thinking about my exotic foreigner, I thought about that last letter I wrote. I saw you, as clear as you are standing here now, reading my letter… and now here you are."

We embrace and kiss and our bodies merged as completely as in the most intense sexual embrace.

"I could love you. I know how to love a man. I would share my home with you, my bed, my food and wine, and my life." She smiles. "I'm happy and content. I can share the happiness with you. However, you must bring your own contentment."

She looks down, "I have had my share of grief, but I have learned to look forward, and not dwell in the sorrow. When I feel sorrow, I look for a glimpse of beauty and it brings my spirits up. A few days ago my hip was hurting too much to walk along the beach. I was feeling sorrow, I really love my walks. As I was drinking my coffee, I looked over the top of the cup at one of my aloe cactus plants. The sun was focused on a new leaf, a perfect shape of gentle curves, shades of new growth green from yellow green to dark green to green bordered with a thin line of red. I smiled. If I had gone for my walk, I would never have seen this beauty. By evening, the new leaf had settled into an ordinary, drab green cactus leaf along with its neighbors. It was a gift, and I try to look for and experience these gifts."

We walk along in silence for a moment.

She turns to me, "Go back now. I know your knee is hurting. Decide...stay or go. My life is good, I'm content. Either way will work for me." She kisses my cheek and walks down the beach.

I'm standing at the threshold of my room. Across the room is my luggage on the bench below the window. Outside, through the window, I see my rental car, it has been turned around facing down the drive. Beyond is the beach, stretching away as far as my eyes can see. The images of the past 24 hours sweep over me. On the beach is a tiny figure walking slowly away, so very small, but I know it is Jacqueline. I blink, and look back, she has faded into the mist rolling in from the sea.

FENDER WASHERS

Bang bang bang BANG! I glance in the rearview mirror and see the left fender of the U-Haul trailer is cracked and loose. We are towing a trailer from San Francisco to southwest Kansas. My daughter, a new teenage driver, has been enjoying using her license. She has wanted to drive more than half of the time. The interstate highway through the Sierra Mountains, across the desert, and over the Rockies had been a good ride. But the north-south highways are rough here in the high, dusty Eastern Colorado plains. It is very dry and sparsely settled. I'm afraid the fender will break off and damage the tire. Not a good place for a breakdown.

I slow down until we arrive at the next town. Main street is wide and dusty with very few cars. The windows of many of the stores are covered with plywood, a common sight in small, western towns.

"Hey Dad," says my daughter, "There's a parking space in front of a hardware store."

We get out and stretch. I feel tension from driving with the broken fender. Opening the door, a small bell rings. It takes a few moments for our eyes to adjust from the bright sunshine outdoors, to the dark interior of the store. I wonder if they are open. At first, I don't see the young man behind the counter.

A voice from the darkness, "Can I help you?"

"I have a cracked fender, and thought I could use two washers," I explain, "and a bolt to hold the broken parts together—"

"Oh, you need a fender washer," he says, before I finish.

I thought he was trying to be funny, and I answer with, "Yeah, right."

He turns, and from shelves stacked to the ceiling with small boxes, he pulls out a box labeled;

FENDER WASHERS

1 1/2 and 2 inch

In all my years I had never seen a fender washer or even heard the word. In his hand he's holding a relatively large metal disc with a small, 1/4 inch hole in the center. I ask the clerk why he had such a large selection of washers.

"We don't get much of a call for them anymore but in the 1930s during the dust bowl, people loaded up Model A Fords with all their belongings and headed west." He hands me two of the bright shinny discs. "The fenders were often old and needed a quick repair. Like I said, not much call for them today."

I look around the store to see what they sell. No plastic wrapped hardware parts, just shelves and shelves and boxes and boxes, all neatly labeled. At the end of the counter is a large metal box on legs, painted with faded red and white Coca-Cola graphics. The corners are rounded. A bottle opener is mounted at one corner; below sits an old coffee can to catch the bottle caps. I lift the lid and select a bottle of Coke awash in melted ice water. My daughter asks for an orange drink so I pick up a Fanta. Returning to the counter, I ask the clerk what I owe; it comes to less than 60 cents. I place a dollar bill on the counter, "Keep the change," I say.

I finish the Coke and as I scoop up the assembled hardware, including an extra set just in case, the clerk asks if I have a screwdriver and pliers. I shake my head. Without hesitation, he opens a drawer below the counter, selects some tools, and heads out the door. By the time I get to the trailer, the young man has already clamped together the broken parts of the fender with the two washers.

"There, that should get you to Kansas," he says. "You outta get off this asphalt state highway and get on the county road. Go east about two miles, then turn south. It's just sand, but it's in better shape. The state doesn't maintain the asphalt out here, but the county does a good job on our local roads."

I thank him, knowing that to offer him money would be insulting his help. I can see some clouds building to the southeast.

"Do you think we'll get some rain?" I ask. I'm concerned about driving on an unpaved road.

"Naw," says the clerk. "That's just a tease. We haven't had rain for six weeks, and then it was only three-hundredths." Looking west at the mountains in the distance, he says, "The Rockies suck out all the moisture from the westerlies, and we're not in line for the winds out of the south that can sometimes bring moisture up from the Gulf." With a shake of his head he adds, "Pretty dry here."

I nod my head.

"I noticed your California plates," he says. "Are you all moving back to Kansas?"

"No," I reply. "We're taking my father's headstone to his grave site." A look of confusion appears on his face, so I add, "I'm a stone carver, and I carved my father's monument myself."

I toss the extra washers into the cup holder, and slide into the driver's seat.

"I want to try out the trailer on the sand road," I tell my daughter.

"How is it different?' she asks.

I try to explain, but not very well. "I'll show you, and try to demonstrate as I drive," I say.

The country road is a pleasure to drive: no more banging fender, no more rough and broken asphalt, and even the car tires give off a gentle sound from the sand. Off to the right are the distant blue shapes of the Rockies. To the left the high, flat prairie stretches as far as the eye can see to the east until it disappears in the curve of the earth. We both need to take a break. There have been no cars on the road, so I pull to the side. My daughter goes off to check out a cactus with a bright yellow flower, and I examine the repair of the fender.

Soon we are on our way again.

"I'm glad you called yourself a stone carver and not a sculptor. I think it would have confused the guy even more," my daughter says. She turns in the seat, looking at me, our eyes meet.

"Hey Dad, how do you get ideas for your sculptures?"

This inquiry is often raised in the classes I teach on stone carving, asked by students trying to make contact with their muse.

"The ideas just come to me," I reply. "I just see them. It's not like looking at a photo or drawing, I see them in the round." I think for a minute. "It's hard to explain. I see them totally, I see them from all different angles at the same time. Sometimes I'm even on the inside myself, feeling the sculpture, feeling the emotion that I'm sculpting."

I pause for a moment. "That's why I can't, and don't draw…. It's impossible to render in two dimensions all that I'm perceiving."

"Yep," replies my daughter, "Good thing you didn't call yourself a sculptor. The guy would have been even more confused."

I laugh.

*   *   *

The call came in about 3:00 AM.

"Your father has just crossed over," my mother said.

We spent a few minutes crying and comforting each other. He had been ill for a few months, and we had known his death was near. In fact, I had been to see him only a few days before. I had reassured him that it was okay to cross over, and it seemed that now was the time. I reminded Dad of what Ram Das had said: "Death is the greatest adventure of all…That is why it is saved until last."

During the phone call, my mother asked me to sculpt the headstone. She thought it should be big enough to also mark her grave in the future.

"You know, your father wanted to return to the soil of western Kansas." After a pause she added, "Oh yes, I guess there should be a cross… all headstones have crosses."

In my mind I see a cross pressing out from behind a veil.

*   *   *

At the grave site, my daughter and I wrestle the stone out of the trailer with pry bars and rollers. The stone weighs 700 pounds. It's hard work, but we manage to place the marker. A discreet distance away, six or eight of my relatives stand in a semi-circle. The men all wear tractor caps with the logos of their favorite farm equipment emblazoned on the front (green caps with John Deere, red with Allis Chalmers, and New Holland on yellow caps). All the men have the face of a farmer: deep red-brown cheeks and ears, but below the cap visor a very white forehead. The women wear long-sleeved dresses and a hat for protection from the sun. No one offers to help, knowing that they would be in the way, and that if I needed help I would ask. All the men and some of the women have their arms crossed over their chests, having never seen anything like this, a carved headstone. My daughter loads the tools in the back of the car.

My mother arrived last night, flying from Seattle to Wichita and driving west for three hours in a rental car. She speaks to the group about the symbolism in the stone carving.

"On the right side, the side of my husband's grave," she says, "the right hand reaches up to the sky. On the left side, the feminine side, the left hand reaches down over the edge of the stone and touches the soil." Mother explains that Dad had wanted to be buried in the soil of the land where she herself had been born and raised, and would return someday. This was home for him. She quotes some Scripture. Still the arms are crossed.

At that moment, the sun shines out from behind a cloud and the faint cross carved between the two outstretched hands becomes obvious.

"Do you all see the cross?" Mother asks.

I had carved the cross as if it were placed behind a veil, and now the bright sun reveals its existence. The arms of the relatives uncross and come down, I hear sounds of surprise.

"There it is," exclaims an aunt, "I see it."

Everyone takes a step or two closer to get a better view of what is now acceptable. Excitement fuels their comments. Like my mother said, "All grave markers have crosses."

I look around, trying to understand what my relatives have just experienced. A few months earlier at my father's burial I had studied where the sun would be in relation to the sculpture. When I created the headstone, I carved the cross to remain hidden except in bright sunlight.

I doubt if any of my relatives have ever seen an outdoor sculpture other than possibly in a photograph where the lighting is fixed. The movement of light over the surface of a sculpture, highlighting certain details and leaving others in shadow brings a sculpture to life. I hope they can allow the symbolism carved in stone to speak. Around the graveyard all the monuments are rectangular blocks of red or black or gray granite. They all look similar in the sun light; dark and somber. With no carvings on their flat surfaces, the movement of sunlight makes very little difference. Over at the edge of our group, mostly in the shade of a cotton wood tree, sits the U-Haul trailer. Only the left fender is in the sun. Like the granite markers, the fender is also dark and rectangular, but on the top is a bright shiny disc, almost blinding in the sunlight… My fender washer.

*   *   *

After the service my mother, my daughter, and I will go to my mother's old home. We stand outside to hear stories of her growing up. The house, once a fine example of early 1900s Prairie Gothic, has almost collapsed. Birds and other wildlife live there now. The collapsed roof allows the rain and winter snow to do their damage. Termites have all but destroyed the main structural timbers. But there is still enough house left to anchor the stories of growing up on the wind-swept prairies of western Kansas. Stories which must be told and passed on to the next generations. I have heard many of the tales, and have experienced some of them myself.

This home was a solid, familiar grounding for me as I grew up. It was where we went for vacations and holidays. We all lived on the farm for six months around my ninth birthday when my dad relocated for a new job. My grandpa taught me to drive a pickup truck, my grandma taught me to bake biscuits, and my uncle from across the road taught me to milk a cow. The memories go on and on.

I know it will be hard for my mother, having just experienced the placing of the monument marking the end of her husband's life, and now experiencing the end of her childhood home. Most likely, there will be only one more return trip for her to Kansas, and that in a box.

Tomorrow, my mother will return to Seattle by the way of a long drive to the airport in Wichita. My daughter and I will drive to Dodge City to return the U-Haul trailer. On the way we will stop at my mother's farmland, land which gave me summer employment during high school and college. Land so flat a person can stand anywhere in a square field, a mile on each side, and can see all four corners. I will wonder if my daughter has any reaction to this land which meant so much to me, but for her there is no direct connection. We will walk out into the field to feel the soil with our feet. The wind will stir the green and golden ripening wheat into rolling waves, swirling away to the north. We'll be surrounded by the sounds and smells of growing wheat.

From Dodge City we'll head southwest to Santa Fe. A roadmap called INDIAN COUNTRY shows all the pueblos and other points of interest. It will be a good guide to Canyon de Chelly, with its ruins of ancient cliff dwellers. Also, to the majestic sculptural forms of Arches National Monument, and later to Meteor Crater. My daughter is a good driver; I will be able to put my seat back and take a nap. And when we return to San Francisco, my daughter will return to her life as a teenager, and I will discover, in the bottom of the cup holder, my fender washers.

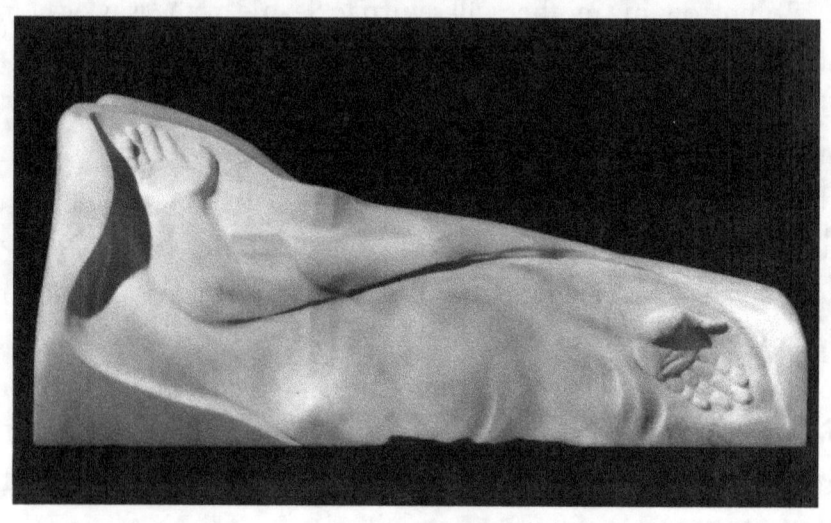

Rotz Family Headstone
Carrara marble, 24 by 48 inches.
Right hand (male) reaching for the sky.
Left hand (female) touching the earth.
Placed in SW Kansas, mother's home.
by Welton Rotz
1986

THAT LOOK

My girlfriend and I decided to live together and create a home. She wanted a dog, I did not. We were pushing 40, I knew dogs come and go, I did not want to go through that again. The next weekend we went to the Colosseum to the Dog Show. After about an hour of barking and dog smells, I said I would meet her in the car. On my way out, next to the exit, was the most beautiful dog I had ever seen. A Finnish Spitz, about 40 pounds, with "prick" ears, curly tail, and a long silky coat of various shades of cinnamon. I went down on my knee. After a little lick on my outstretched hand, he put one paw on my thigh and gave me another little kiss. His eyes were black, totally deep, deep black. Not like the yellow or brown eyes of other dogs. It looked as if he had applied mascara above and below his eyes and carried the black line out to the side. When I touched him, he was as soft as ground cinnamon. The next week we went to Sacramento to pick out a puppy and a few weeks later we returned to bring our puppy home.

We were sitting on our haunches on the floor and the breeder brought out the puppy and his mother. They played tug toy together for a while, the mother very gentle, letting the pup win. When the pup tired, he just fell asleep on the floor between her paws. The breeder said it was now time to go. She placed the sleeping pup in the crook of my right arm. His mother stood on my bent knees and gave her pup a few little licks. She knew that this was the last puppy to leave home, and maybe even her last litter. I cupped my left hand under her chin, and she gave my wrist a little lick. I bent and kissed her head. Her eyes with that dark deep black looked up at me. With a whisper as clear as could be she said,

"Please, take care of my son."

And she gave me THAT LOOK.

So the puppy moved in and became a part of our home. And then he moved on as did the next and the next, the memories of them fading into the mist of time. Which one loved to come and jump in bed with us in the morning, sharing in the love and the warmth? Which one enjoyed hiking in the high Sierra, and taking a swim in the ice-cold mountain lakes? Which one enjoyed going sailing, rushing ahead down the dock and jumping aboard the boat, waiting for the sails to be raised and our casting off? Which one enjoyed long walks on the beach, dashing ahead to scatter the seagulls, then proudly running back to us splashing through the surf? Perhaps it was all of them.

So why are these memories coming back to me at this time, coming faster that I can write them down?

Last night I had to get up at 3 am. In the dim light as I sat on the edge of the bed I reached out with my left hand to find the handle of my walker, now a necessary aid for me to even go to the bathroom. There was her face, her head cupped in my hand. Her eyes glowing from their deep darkness as vivid as they had forty years ago. We looked at each other for a moment.

"Thank you, they were all my puppies," she said.

As she faded away, she again gave me

THAT LOOK

VERY BLACK HEART

"Why are we here?" I shout at the professor. "What the hell are we doing in this place?"

The professor squirms on the bench seat in the hall. Two other interns sit beside him.

Before he can answer, John, our fourth member, comes out of the room and sits a few spaces away. His elbows on his knees, his face buried in his hands, he cries. Moving over to him, I place my arm around his shoulders. No words are spoken.

John, the only married member of our intern group, has a toddler and a new baby. It is hard to imagine the agony he experienced in that room. A room containing 40 small beds, each raised to about waist high, with short side boards, not as tall as a crib's. And in each bed lay a small human child. Some with missing body parts, a few with a shape so grotesque they looked more like a creature from the deep sea, and there was the one with the very small body and the head so large... I couldn't go on. I had to leave the room.

"I see that you're upset," says the professor in his best therapeutic voice. "You are here at the state hospital as interns, to see what's out there in the world. Someday, when you are the pastor of a church, and a member of your congregation gives birth to a misshapen child, today's experience may help you give the family your steady pastoral care."

"I could do without it," I say.

*　*　*

The tuberculosis test comes back positive. This means I can do my next intern work at the local TB hospital. Having lived in southeast Asia as a child, I was exposed to enough TB germs to have built up immunity.

Going down the long halls of the hospital, if there is a door open, I ask the patient if they would like a visit. In my suit pocket is a small copy of the New Testament, but I carry no other religious materials. My mission (if I may call it that) is to "visit the sick."

Most of the people I visit with are bored. Even family members cannot spend much time in the hospital. I often feel uncomfortable being a seminary student. What can I offer them? Some patients know more Scripture than I do, and they ask me to read the Bible to them, as if I had some special connection.

What I learned from this internship was how boring a stay in a hospital could be.

"Visit the sick, feed the hungry, and clothe the naked," were Jesus's words. If I ever become a minister, "visiting the sick" will be an important part of my job.

*　*　*

One summer as a teenager working on my uncle's farm, at a breakfast table discussion, I accidentally (on purpose) misquoted Jesus.

"Didn't Jesus tell us," I say. "To feed the hungry, clothe the sick, and visit the naked."

My cousin, having just taken a big gulp of milk, let go with a laugh/cough, spewing milk all over his plate and half the table. My uncle did not think it was funny.

*　*　*

"There's something special tonight," says one of the medical interns at San Francisco General Hospital's Psychiatric Ward.

"What is it?" I ask. I'm on my last intern assignment.

"I don't know," he answers. "But it must be something special, just look at the size of the intern group."

I have observed from 10:30 pm to 1:30 am every Friday night for six weeks. This is the most active time. I have observed the clean up, with a water hose and long-handled scrub brush, of those people brought in off the streets. I only needed to watch this once.

Tonight, as usual, the staff doctor starts his rounds about 12:30 am.

He stops at each patient, looks at the chart hanging on the end of the bed, walks up to the side of the bed and greets the person laying there. I am continually impressed by how the doctor touches each one. For some he shakes their hand, others he places his hand on their shoulder, or on top of their head.

A few weeks ago, one of the medical interns asked the doctor why he touches each patient.

"You can learn a great deal by touching," answered the doctor.

We arrive at the last bed. The doctor follows the routine: the chart, the greeting, and the touching.

"Have you something special to show us?" asks the doctor.

The man jumps out of bed, excitedly pulls up his gown with one hand, and holds out his penis with the other.

There, on the head of his penis is tattooed a very black heart. We all react with a gasp or moan.

The only woman intern in the group expresses out loud what each man is feeling. "OH MY GOD, that must've hurt like hell!"

We all lean in to get a better look.

"Okay," says the doctor. "Thank you. You can get back in bed now."

The old man, maybe 70, drops the edge of his gown, turns and crawls into bed. He curls up in a fetal position. His 15 minutes of fame is over.

Tonight, the rounds have finished later than usual. I leave after 2:00 am. My last night as an intern is complete.

I drive home through the dark streets of San Francisco. In the distance I hear a siren. I wonder if someone is being taken to S.F. General Hospital.

The early morning hours of a dark night are prime for introspection and reflection.

"What have I learned tonight as an intern?" I ask myself. "What have I learned in the course on Pastoral Counseling?" The ever-present question festering just below the surface of my mind raises its ugly head again.

"Have I chosen the right profession?"

There's no answer yet.

Already, in the early 1960s, there are signs that something is not right within the Church. Attendance and membership are down. Students and even faculty are leaving other seminaries to join San Francisco Theological Seminary where there is a very loud focus on making the Church "relevant." They, as I, desire to be a part of this social awakening. This exciting time can best be expressed in the words on S.F.T.S. President Theodore Gill's memorial, set in place more than 50 yeas later, remembering the early 1960s:

He welcomed world-class teachers, learners, storytellers, dramatists, musicians, and other artists to this campus. In words and actions, Ted Gill inspired a whole generation of students.

"For this is theological education: bumping into, shaking out, trying to make sense of real issues—not just the familiar, safe, traditional questions long propounded to keep abstract intellects pleasantly engaged, but the real thumpers, the tough ones, the disquiets and dissembling and distempers that matter, that make a present difference in this, God's earth, God's time, to these, God's people"

But is there a dark, black heart in some hidden private part of my psyche telling me to rethink my alignment with the Church?

It is still dark when I arrive home from the hospital internship, but first light is coming soon. As I said, "The dark of night is a good time for reflection." Maybe the light of the new day will give some "reflection," some illumination, to the old question.

SELMA MONTGOMERY MARCH

March 21, 1965

"I ain't never seen a white man hiking bales," the old black farmer said.

"Phew, these two wire bales are nothing," I replied, loading a hay bale into his truck with a pair of hay hooks. "One summer I was working on the farm. We were hauling three wire straw bales for the new Interstate Highway."

"Oh my," the farmer replied, "they must have weighed seventy... seventy-five pounds!"

"Right," I answered. "My job was to walk along beside the truck and pick up bales and pass them up to the crew on the truck."

The old man just shook his head.

"And what's more," I said, "we kept an extra pair of hay hooks in a bucket of water, 'cause I was working so fast the metal hay hooks were getting hot and we didn't want to catch the straw on fire."

The old man looked at me for a long minute, then sat down on the last bale and laughed. I sat next to him and joined in.

It was good to laugh. The day before had been no laughing matter. This was the second day of the Selma Montgomery March in the spring of 1965. It feels very strange to tell this story now more than sixty years later, but it needs to be told.

It was raining and the field we were to camp in overnight was wet. As we set up the tents, an old black farmer had come up and offered some hay bales to open and spread around inside the tents. But he needed help to load his pickup truck. The bales were too heavy for him. I volunteered. Arriving at his barn, I saw that the bales were hay, not straw.

"What about feeding your livestock?" I asked.

"I only got two old mules left," he replied. "Winter's over, and they be on pasture now."

We loaded the bales in the pickup.

When he and I returned to the camp site with our load of hay, the marchers were just arriving, followed by a big Red Cross mobile unit. Even though it was raining, and everyone was tired and wet, the marchers were singing;

We shall overcome. We shall overcome.
Deep in my heart, I do believe
We shall overcome,
Someday

The Red Cross bus had a bullet hole in the side.

As I write this today, so many years later, with all the killings and racial violence that are an almost daily occurrence, I wonder if we did any good going to Selma. I was a student, age twenty-four, at San Francisco Theological Seminary, preparing to go into the Presbyterian ministry. Those were heady times for the church. There was much sharing of ideas between different schools, and opposing denominations; Protestant, Catholic, and Jewish. San Francisco Theological Seminary was leading the way on many fronts. Students and faculty from other schools in the East were transferring to our school to be in on the new excitement. "Relevant" was the buzz word of the time. We were looking for ways to make the church's teachings relevant to the world. And going to Selma seemed, at the time, to be relevant.

We had arrived in Selma after a forty-hour bus ride, stopped at Brown's Chapel after dark (as planned for our safety), and carried our duffels inside. It was lit by only a few bulbs high in the ceiling. The walls were covered with beautiful wood trim, stained very dark as was the style in 1908. The dark wood seemed to suck away any extra light. Down front, to the left was a 4' X 8' sheet of plywood. Its new, raw wood was in strong contrast to the old, dark wood trim in the room. It covered a broken stained-glass window. We learned that after the first march, some police had been chasing two or three little girls. The girls ran into the church to find sanctuary. The police followed, grabbed the little girls and threw them through the glass window. Welcome to Selma. I tried to make myself comfortable, stretched out on the pews, using a hymnal from the pew rack for a pillow. I drifted off to sleep wondering what was ahead for us.

I awoke early for the first day of the march. Some of our group joined those marching. I volunteered to help make up a work crew to set up the evening camp sites. We loaded materials and supplies into a few pickups, climbed aboard and headed in the direction of Montgomery. The marchers were ahead of us by about an hour. As we drove across the Edmund Pettus Bridge, my thoughts were on the terrible beatings that had taken place here only a few weeks before. I wondered if we too would be met with violence.

The first attempt had been March 7, 1965. It was met with tear gas, police clubs, and dogs. The march was turned back. A second march, on the 9th, was also turned back. Later that day, a minister from Massachusetts, James Reed, was beaten by KKK members, and died. Dr. Martin Luther King Jr., had called his friend and fellow theologian Dr. Theodore Gill, President of SFTS, and said that there needed to be more white faces on the next march.

So here we were, starting out again to Montgomery on the 21st.

The site for the first night's camp was a cow pasture…which had had cows grazing in it only a few days before. The field was about the size of three basketball courts. Our first job was to clean up the cow pies and dump them over the fence. A crew of carpenters, organized by the march committee were busily constructing a wooden stage and setting up the portable toilets. Our job was to help erect the two circus tents contracted for the march. A large truck with the tents arrived, the old driver got out and limped back to his load. He showed us how to unroll and stretch out the canvas. Driving the tent stakes was next, then raising the tent poles. With all of us pulling and lifting, the poles went up carrying the canvas tent up with them. We tied the ropes to the tent stakes, adjusted the tension, and the tents were ready; one for sleeping and one for food service.

The local Sears and Roebuck store, in support of the march, had given the organizers any materials and equipment they might need. A gasoline driven electrical generator, coils of wire, along with other supplies had been dropped off at the camp site. No one seemed to know what to do with the generator, so I took on the job. We carefully buried 100 feet of wire from the stage to a location as far away as possible. The wire was out of sight, no danger of tripping people in the dark, and the pasture was not destroyed by the digging.

As soon as the stage was built, the construction crew moved on. When the tents were erected, their owner left saying he would be back in the morning. Shortly after the job of burying the electrical wire was finished, the air was filled with the thumping roar of a helicopter coming in. Everyone scattered. The aircraft with its Air National Guard markings hovered about five feet off the ground. Six or eight men jumped out, dressed in full battle gear, surrounded the ship, flopped on the ground with their rifles pointing out. More men jumped out, taking up kneeling positions behind the first group, their rifles at ready. Gear was thrown out and the helicopter took off.

While most of the soldiers stayed in battle positions, a small group started scanning the ground with a metal detector. I approached them.

"Get back!" they shouted. "We're clearing the area of possible mines."

I shouted back, "We have been over this whole field picking up cow shit."

Just then they came upon the buried electrical wire. Their metal detector started to scream.

"That's an electric wire we buried," I shouted. "See, one end is at the stage and the other is over there at the generator."

With this, the Guardsmen regrouped and set up six camp sites around the perimeter of our field, just outside the pasture fence.

Evidently, before this march, Dr. King had talked directly with President Johnson and said that there would be a blood bath if the National guard did not show up at the march…and it would be on the President's hands. For us, having crossed the Edmund Pettus Bridge with no violence, and working for a day on the marcher's night camp with no one in sight, I was wondering if this display of military might was a bit much.

As dusk set in, we could see the Guardsmen sites just beyond the pasture fence. Farther out in the swamps were at least ten campsites, most likely occupied by local, Lowndes County good ol' boys. As we settled to sleep that night, I was thinking and feeling the question: "Was tonight the night we would be shot at, burned out, or otherwise killed?" I offered a prayer of thanks for the National Guard.

Just two and a half days before, we left SFTS early in the morning. The seminary community had gathered together to send us off for the forty-hour bus ride to Selma. We formed a circle, joined hands, and sang some hymns. The last song was "Kumbaya."

The bus ride became tedious. As the miles rolled on, I spent time thinking, as did the others, were we going to our deaths?

It was light when our bus rolled through Tennessee. My maternal great grandmother was born and raised on a cotton plantation in Tennessee. Her father owned slaves. After the Civil War, at age eighteen, my great grandmother, her two brothers, and her new husband (her former school teacher) left Tennessee. Their home and life on the plantation was in ruins, destroyed in the war. The four young folks headed to that golden promised land of California. They traveled west in a wagon pulled by two mules, and made it as far as central Kansas. My mother, Clara, remembered asking her grandma, Clara,

"Why did you stop in Kansas?"

"That's where the mule went lame," the old lady replied.

Here I am, my great grandmother's "Someday." I have made it to California, and now I am going the other way, back to the South to do what I can to right the wrongs of that time.

After the march, and returning to SFTS, I created a sculpture of a person stepping over a partially buried tear gas canister. The canister had been brought back by one of the students who was on the bridge for the first march, and had been beaten and gassed. In the sculpture, the person's hands are raised, clapping, his head tipped back singing. Singing was what kept the spirit of the march going. With sore feet, or rain, or fear, and even joys, old songs were sung and new songs were composed. A favorite was "Keep Your Eyes on The Prize (Hold On)." With hands free, we clapped the syncopated rhythm. These songs were no "Kumbaya," but gut expressions about the governor and the sheriff of Lowndes County, and the unstoppable need to be free. The words were about transcending oppression despite any struggles that may arise. Each day new verses were created and added. Our seminary group was recognized with:

> *I'm gonna board that big Greyhound*
> *Carry the love from town to town*
> *Keep your eyes on the prize, hold on.*

Later, in the spring, at graduation I gave the sculpture to President Dr. Theodore Gill. He in turn gave it to the Seminary. I did not graduate. I never returned to seminary. In the months that followed that graduation, very upsetting actions were happening within SFTS. Hundreds of millions of dollars were lost when longtime donors of the seminary withdrew their support.

Their reason: the seminary's involvement in civil rights. SFTS almost collapsed. President Dr. Theodore Gill was "promoted" to a small, windowless office in New York City. He was not allowed to speak out about this action of the church. The sculpture I had created with the teargas canister was removed from its prominent location in the library. The maintenance men were told to destroy the sculpture. Instead, they placed it out of sight, way in the back of a very tall cupboard. A year or so later, I was told where the sculpture was hidden. I rescued it and sent it off to the original owner of the canister.

I guess the church was not as forward thinking, or as relevant, as it claimed to be.

At the fifty-year reunion of the march, attended by maybe fifteen or twenty, many memories and stories were shared. Dr. Theodore Gill Jr., President Gill's son, now a prestigious theologian in Switzerland, filled us in on many of the details of his father's final years. I said that I would like to donate a sculpture to the seminary in honor of President Gill. SFTS had changed in those fifty years; there were woman's study courses, and classes on racial issues. I felt it fitting to honor Dr. Gill's vision.

The sculpture was installed two years later with the help of the then-president. It is a seven-foot-tall slab of black granite with a very highly polished oval on the surface of the slab. As a person looks at the sculpture… and into the sculpture, one's image is reflected back darkly. The title:

THROUGH A GLASS DARKLY,
based on 1 Corinthians 13:12

The bronze plaque reads:

Rev. Dr. Theodore A. Gill
President of SFTS 1958 - 1966

...he welcomed world-class teachers, learners, story-tellers, dramatists, musicians, and other artists to this campus. In words and actions, Ted Gill inspired a whole generation of students.

For this is theological education: bumping into, shaking out, trying to make sense of real issues—not just the familiar, safe, traditional questions long propounded to keep abstract intellects pleasantly engaged, but the real thumpers, the tough ones, the disquiets and dissembling and distempers that matter, that make a present difference in this, God's earth, God's time, to these, God's people.

The plaque continues, mentioning Dr. Gill's many involvements, including his "controversially accompanying students and staff to join Dr. Martin Luther King Jr. in the 1965 voting rights march from Selma to the capital in Montgomery, Alabama."

At the fifty-year reunion, I recalled the last night of the march. We were in the outskirts of Montgomery in an Olympic-sized athletic field. Thousands of people showed up to join in the festivities. Some brought their station wagons or pickups with food to share. Some celebrities came, including the cast of BONANZA, in their western costumes. Harry Belafonte and Lena Horne were also there, not to entertain, but to add their support to the march and the voter registration movement.

Early the next morning we lined up for the final march to the capital. Dr. King and Dr. Gill at the front. Our group of seminarians were to make up the second line, but eager people kept crowding in. By the time we started, our group was about five or six lines back. As the day progressed, we kept being moved back and back. It was okay with me, I had no desire to be in the front if there was violence. The route of the march progressed through a very poor part of the capital city. The locals cheered us.

The next neighborhood was slightly better, but the people were what was called "white trash." We were booed. The men seemed to all wear white T-shirts, a pack of cigarettes rolled up in their short sleeves. It was here I thought there might be violence. Walking along the outside of the marchers was a group of very big, very muscular young black men dressed uniformly in new, dark blue denim overalls. They kept the marchers in line, leaving plenty of room between them and the curb. This also gave the men room to move forward or back along the march to be the first to meet any aggression from bystanders. The march had been organized very well.

As we progressed, the march often stopped. I could not see why, but at one stop, I ran ahead to a small store to buy some candy. At the checkout line, the man in front of me was huge. His neck went straight down from his ears to his shoulders to disappear in his tight T-shirt. The neck was bright red, sun burned red. A real, southern "red neck." Behind me was another. I was very uneasy. Outside the store, the march had started to move. The young, blond man at the checkout counter, leaned over to me as he counted out my change. He said in a very soft voice, "Thanks for coming."

We could see the capital in the distance, our goal. The street widened out, as did the marchers, and our group made it to the front as we arrived at the steps to the capital building. The Alabama state police were in a line across the steps, rifles and shotguns at their side at parade rest. Dr. King stepped forward and called out to the governor by name. The speeches began. We settled in to listen to this historic moment.

Very soon however, the march organizer came to us and said that it was time to go…our job was done. We had succeeded in helping to get the march to the capital steps. I was relieved, sorry to miss the speeches, but mostly tired. Our group boarded a railroad train chartered to take us the fifty-four miles back to Selma. The train pulled into a siding just outside of town to let us off. There was concern that we might meet violence if the train rolled into the center of town. We walked through a residential area of Selma, every house was dark. All lights were out. The only lights in town were a single bulb overhead in the center of each intersection. Below each light stood a lone National Guardsman in full battle dress.

The adrenaline was pumping through my tired body. I was thinking, *So close to the end, but not quite there.* To our great relief, the big Greyhound bus was waiting at the church for us. We ran in and grabbed our duffels which we had left behind only a few days, but a lifetime before. We didn't even take the time to change into clean clothes, but ran to the bus. The driver, very eager to get going, slammed the doors closed as soon as possible, and asked where we wanted to go. We all shouted, "San Francisco!"

"Oh, no, we gotta go somewhere in the South," The driver said. "How about New Orleans?"

He scrolled up the destination marker on the front of the bus to indicate our supposed destination. He also told us to keep the interior lights off.

Once the bus left Selma that night, we all tried to relax. The adrenaline had left us exhausted and we tried to sleep. The march was over and we were on our way home. With each mile the bus put us farther away from the feared violence that had been with us for the whole time. We settled in for the forty-hour bus ride home. At 7:00 am the next morning, someone tuned to the news on a portable radio. It was mostly about Vietnam, something we had almost forgotten about. At the end of the news, the announcer said,

"This is just in. Last night a car with out-of-state license plates was found in a ditch outside Montgomery, Alabama. The car was registered to a Mrs. Viola Liuzzo, of Detroit, Michigan. The body of a white woman was in the car. She was killed by multiple gun shots through the driver's side window."

A cold pain slammed through my gut. I felt sick. We all had thought that we and the other marchers and the leaders had escaped the feared violence. I was crying. Someone started in a quavering voice:

We shall overcome. We shall overcome.
Deep in my heart, I do believe
We shall overcome,
Someday

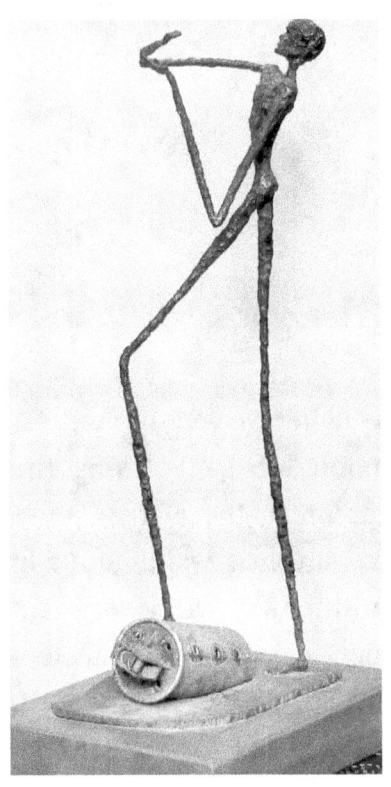

We Shall Over Come
22 inches tall
Teargas canister and steel
Welton Rotz
1965

GRANDMA

The bright morning light revealed the face was crooked.

Yesterday afternoon I began carving the face on the gray Bardiglio marble figure of the Dark Goddess. The rest of the marble sculpture was finished, waiting for a final polish. The soft, northern light from the high window began to fade, but I kept working even though it became difficult to see. I had not been concerned that the face was left undone. I trusted that when the right time came along, my muse would help me create the carving. I kept working until dark.

Now, the next day, I see that the face is asymmetrical…crooked. I pick up my carving tool and approach the misshapen face.

"NO!" comes a voice loud enough to hear over the electric grinder.

"That's the way it is…leave it be."

A cold chill flashes through my body.

I drop the tool.

Goose bumps stand up on my bare arms.

The marble sculpture seems to dissolve. My maternal grand-mother is standing there. She has that sweet, funny lopsided smile which we all loved. When she was sixteen, she was kicked in the face by a mule. Her jaw never healed correctly. She could smile, eat, and talk without difficulty, but one was always aware that her face was not symmetrical. That was grandma.

She had been a wonderful, loving presence in my early life. She taught me how to make biscuits, using just the right sized water glass to cut out the shape from the rolled out dough.

Frying pancakes was her specialty. The griddle had to be the correct temperature. She showed me how to wet my hand, then shake a splatter of drops on the hot surface. Too hot, and the water drops flashed away. Too cold, the water just puddled up. Just right, the drops sputtered and danced on the griddle surface. Watch the bubbles and turn only once. Perfect pancakes: golden brown, light, and fluffy.

One morning coming in from before-breakfast chores, I noticed the early light was different. I had often watched the sun rise, but this day the night dew had settled on the bearded heads of wheat, and each head sparkled in the clear early light. I ran into the kitchen.

"Grandma," I said, "come quick, I want to show you something!"

Without hesitating, she turned off the fire under the pancakes and came outside with me. From the porch, we could see the prairie flat fields of ripening wheat stretching to the east. Just as the sun peeked over the horizon there was a flash of solar energy shooting towards us, and passing on by, traveling almost faster than the eye could see, the light reflected by the billions and billions of dew drops.

Grandma hugged me and kissed the top of my head.

"Thanks for showing me," she said. "I've lived here over 40 years and have never seen the light of the sunrise traveling over the land, over the face of the earth."

We turned and entered the kitchen. The pancakes were overdone and dumped into the slop pail under the sink. Later, the chickens would enjoy the scorched breakfast.

*   *   *

In my workshop, the image of my grandma fades and the sculpture remains. I see her eternal beauty in the face. And I see the love she gave me and the world around her. I had not thought of my grandmother for many years after her death. But now I realized this sculpture is not the *Dark Goddess* as I had planned. It is the *Wise Old Woman*.

The old woman is not just standing still. Her right foot is raised to take a step, the toes lifting the hem of her garments. On the back, the heel of her left foot is up about an inch, again the hem is lifted. I sculpt the existing stylized wings of the Goddess to match the flowing garments.

The face…I let it be.

WISE OLD WOMAN- detail
Bardiglio marble, 60 inches tall
By Welton Rotz, circa 1990

WISE OLD WOMAN

Bardiglio marble, 60 inches tall

By Welton Rotz, circa 1990

LET HER KNOW
BEFORE YOU GRAB HER TEATS

I'm carrying one of the two milk pails. It's so cold that I keep changing hands so I can put the other one in my coat pocket. My uncle Hugh is carrying the second pail on our way to the barn.

"Why are the barn doors open?" I ask.

"So the cows can get in out of the cold," Hugh replies.

I guess I was expecting a more profound answer. I'm eight years old and full of questions. My uncle is patient and always has an answer, usually short and to the point.

Sure enough, when we get to the barn, the cows are already inside. They are standing in their accustomed stalls, but turn their heads to look at us and give a welcoming "moooooow." My job is to pour a coffee can full of grain along with a flake of alfalfa hay into the manger in front of each cow. After the cow has put her head through the stocks to reach the food I lock down the stanchion holding her in place.

My uncle has placed a short chain with two large hooks around the hocks of the first cow's lower back legs. This is to keep her from kicking and knocking over the milk pail. He talks to her, telling her what a beautiful girl she is, all the time rubbing his hands over her back and side, to warm them. Working his way down, bending over to caress her udder, he picks up the milk pail, squats on a one-legged stool, and taking a teat in each hand begins to milk. Looking over his shoulder, Hugh tells me I can start on the second cow. In this cold weather, it takes time for the cow to let down her milk, and she needs to be primed.

Hugh has taught me to milk, but today I have by-passed some of the essential beginning steps. I squat down and grab the cow's teats.

It all happens so fast! I'm face down in a pile of fresh cow poop, a good distance behind the cow. She has kicked me. Unlike a horse, who kicks straight back, a cow brings her leg up alongside her body, swings the leg out, then kicks back.

"You okay?" asks my uncle without missing a stroke of his milking. "You need to let her know before you grab her teats."

I haven't milked since I was eight years old, but I have kept this good advice in mind ever since.

VISITOR

"OH CRAP!" Susan shouts. She bangs her hand on the steering wheel of the pickup truck. "Why didn't I check the gas this morning?" *I just want to get through this desolate western Kansas and on to Santa Fe. The fuel gauge light just came on, or has it been on for a while? I may run out of gas any second. Oh, there's a small town... Not much of a town, even the gas station is closed! Hummmm, there's a church with parked cars. I'll just go in and sit in the back until after the service then ask where I can get some gas.*

Susan settles in the back row of the small church. The service is almost over.

"Are there any announcements?" asks the preacher. "Any visitors?"

A few heads turn and look at her.

"Hi, my name is Susan. I'm just passing through on my way to Santa Fe. I'm almost out of gas and wondered where's the closest station?"

"How many miles you got left?" someone asks.

"I don't know."

53

"Can't chance it."

Others join in.

"I've a half gallon in the back of my truck."

"Won't make it." All agree

A man in front of Susan turns.

"Hi." He takes her hand, "My name is David."

Susan tries to respond, but is thinking, *He wants to shake my hand. What big hands he has! Why am I thinking that way? But they feel good, and he doesn't want to let go.*

"I've got some gas you can have," David says. "About three miles down the road, in the direction of Santa Fe. Why don't you follow me? Better yet, I'll have my folks drive my car and I'll ride with you, if that's okay. You know, make sure you make the turn. We're about a quarter mile off the highway." David pauses, then grins. "With that blue blouse you look like an angel. Oh, I'm sorry!"

"I've heard a lot of pickup lines." Susan laughs. "But I've never been called an angel."

"I'm really sorry…." replies David, obviously embarrassed. "Just thinking out loud."

"Why do I look like an angel to you?"

Still embarrassed, David says, "Oh, I'll tell you later…"

Later? As soon as I get some gas, I'm out of here.

"I'll tell my folks. Meet you outside."

In the parking lot, David admires Susan's pickup.

"Wow! What a beautiful pickup! Did you do the paint job? I really like the blue on blue on blue. Different hues and even different textures."

"Yea, well, I didn't do the actual painting, but I did the design," Susan says. *Why is he walking to the driver's side?*

"Oh, sorry…" David stops abruptly. "Just habit."

They climb into the truck and Susan turns out onto the highway. She looks out over the fields. *This highway is so straight, and the land is so flat...*

David breaks the silence. "This land is really flat, isn't it?"

"Yea, just what I was thinking," Susan answers.

Pointing to the left, David says, "Turn here. We're up the road apiece behind those trees... Drive to the back by those large fuel tanks."

"Which tank?" asks Susan.

"This truck take regular? The one on the left," says David.

Susan nods, then asks, "Is this your home?"

David gets out of the truck and starts to fill the tank. "Yes and no, my folks live here. I grew up here, but I have my own place. Sometimes I stay here depending on our work. I often have Sunday dinner here with my folks." He continues, "How about staying for dinner? Mom said to ask you."

"Oh, thanks, but I can't wait for dinner. I've got to get going."

"Dinner is now, mid-day. Supper is the evening meal," David explains, "You got to eat before you hit the road! Mom said she really wants you to stay for dinner."

"OK, I'm pretty hungry," says Susan, surprised, but relieved. "I don't want to impose. Hey, you just filled up my tank. What do I owe you?"

"Nothing, I don't do business on Sunday," David says.

"From your smile I know you're kidding me. Well, thanks! Dinner sounds wonderful!" Susan says. "I'm pretty hungry."

At dinner, Susan explains that she is going to the desert to paint.

"Oh, that's nice..." says David's mother, trying to be a good host. "Like that woman painter, what's her name?"

"Georgia O'Keeffe. She influenced me, but my style is different."

Dinner is going okay, a little awkward, not much conversation.

"I would like to see your work," says David.

"Sorry," Susan says, "It's all wrapped up in the truck." Looking at David, she says, "You look disappointed."

"Yeah."

Susan starts to help clear, but is shooed away by Mom. David and Susan collide in the kitchen doorway. David, a little embarrassed, speaks too loud. "I've got to go across the road and turn on the windmill to fill the stock tank for the cattle. Bet you've never seen a genuine Kansas windmill."

Susan smiles, thinking, *He has a strange sense of humor.*

"Well, okay. I hate to eat and run, and a walk would feel good after this wonderful dinner."

They walk across the road together to the old homestead, past the house, empty now since the grandparents died. Susan is fascinated by the crumbling cream and gray colors of the old house and the faded red and white trim of the barn beyond.

He is very quiet. I know he is thinking what to say.

David stops, looks at the ground.

"Was it the skulls over the desert that O'Keeffe painted that influenced you," he asks. "Or was it the close up of flowers that look like a woman's—ah….well…. you know?"

"Vagina," Susan says. "You can use that word."

Embarrassed, David says, "Yeah, but not in polite company. Sometimes my mouth and my thoughts are out of sync with my polite brain."

"Me too," Susan says. "And then I'm out of sync with the people around me, so I just shut up, and then I feel very lonely."

"LONELY!" David shouts. "You don't know lonely. Look around you, other than my folks, the closest person is at the next homestead two miles away." He looks east. "Then it's the town and you saw how empty that is. No one to talk to, other than about cattle prices and when to plant. Sometimes I feel so god damn lonely I could shoot myself." He supresses a sob, "but then I'm afraid I would be lonely for eternity on the other side.

"I got married right out of high school." Susan takes David's hand. "I thought it would help me get away, but we stayed in the same town. It was awful! Someone once said that the only thing worse than being alone and feeling lonely was to be not alone, and feeling lonely." She looks down. "The marriage lasted a year."

David gives Susan's hand a little squeeze.

"I got a job in a little cafe, cooking and waiting tables," Susan says. "Seems that men think a divorced woman is an easy lay." Looking at David, she says, "Gave up on dating, focused on my job, taking community college classes, and spent a lot of alone time with my painting."

"Yeah, me too," David says, still holding her hand. "I read a lot, listen to music, and take a trip at least once a year." With a quick look, he changes the subject. "Ah! Here's the stock tank and the windmill. See, I just release this lever, the tail up above swings out, and the wind makes the blades go round and round. The well rod goes up and down." He mimics the sound, "Ka lunka dunk, ka lunka dunk, ka lunka dunk, and the well pumps out water from deep underground. Free!" He says with a smile. "I'll get you a drink." He points to an old stoop. "Sit here."

There is something about him, the way he walks, picking up an old mug turned over on top of a fence post, rinsing it out, trying a sip, pouring it out, refilling, and bringing me a mug of water. I seem to be observing, ...no— I'm a part of a ritual, he's making an offering to me. She shakes her head. "David, this whole scene, I mean, the whole world is changing, the colors are more vivid! The ripening wheat, gold, and amber, and tan with a touch of hidden green, swaying in the wind, stretched as far as I can see, the sun at my back. And I haven't even drank of the magical water yet."

"Here," David says, "Try this."

"Oh my god, David! I have never tasted anything like this! No bottled water, no special spring water, it's….it's…."

"It's pretty awesome isn't it?" David smiles. "Worth the experience?"

"Oh yes! What are you doing to me? I want to go to Santa Fe and see how O'Keeffe was able to interpret the light and colors of the desert and then communicate its grandeur to me even though I have never seen the desert. And now you've made me see the grandeur here in this awful, lonely place." Susan takes another sip. "The empty town, the church one-quarter filled, all with gray hair, the old farm buildings falling down, the old rusty machinery rotting away in the pasture." She clenches her fists. "And even your folks seem to have one foot in the grave." Lowering her hands looking at David. "I have never been pregnant, but that wheat, that golden green moving, undulating field seems ready to explode, or to expand, to give birth." She looks up, "What is happening to me David?"

"We start harvest this week. You can feel it," David answers.

Susan feels a sob building and thinks, *I'm crying. I'm finishing the water in the mug.*

David sits next to her, puts his arm around her. "I'll get you more water in a minute." he says.

"What's happening to me?" Susan asks again as she leans into David's support. "I got up this morning, and for the first time on my trip I really felt great. Better than crying all the way across Pennsylvania. I meditated, felt centered, decided to put on fresh clothes."

"Oh yeah," David smiles, "The angel blouse."

"Shhhhh. Usually when I start the day in a good place, the day goes very well. You know, good feelings make for good feelings. Then I ran out of gas."

"Almost."

"Well, okay." Susan nods. *I'm sitting here on this old step, crying. I want to go to Santa Fe. But what is happening to my day?*

"Ain't over yet!" David answers. "Your tears are tears of awe. I have them sometimes too." He glances up. "This morning I was going back to bed and not going to church with my folks. I don't go to church that much, it's more of a social time for most of us farmers, a chance to talk with other people, even if it is about the weather." He stops for a moment. "As I came out of the bathroom, I looked at my collection of blue cobalt glass on my windowsill. The sun was shining through with such intensity! The whole room was blue." He smiles, "I was filled with joy! You see, I believe that I have a spirit that walks with me, kind of like an angel. I have never seen her, I think it is a her, but I see blue things, or blue lights around things, and then I know she is near." David adds, "That explains my comment about your blue blouse."

"Oh," Susan responds, "But what is happening? I don't feel like an angel. It's just me." *He's looking at me like he knows something I don't.*

"I think …I believe that this day is no accident," David says. "The light in my blue glass. You forgetting to check the gas. It has all brought us together." He glances at the windmill. "For me, you have helped me see beyond the loneliness of this dead and dying place. There is life here, I just have to find it. For you, I hope I have in some way helped you, with your artist's eye, see the essence of the world around you. We have a choice: to see the dead and rotting realities around us. Or to see the new, the vital energy, the potential realities. It's a full-time job, every day. I believe life is supposed to be good. But sometimes I forget and get caught up in negative thoughts and feelings." David looks at Susan. "I try to see the best of the world around me and be appreciative, even of the small things. I believe that our thoughts and emotions create—"

Susan interrupts. "But what do we do? I feel kinda rung out."

"Well, you could…uh oh, stock tank is overflowing." David pulls the control lever and turns off the windmill. "Let's head back."

They walk back together in silence. Susan thinks, *I feel empty. But not a bad, lonely emptiness. Maybe it's making room for something new.* "David," Susan says. "I really feel tired, too tired to start driving now. Is there a place I could take a little nap?"

"Yeah, there's a guest room in the back of the house."

Susan slips into the guest bed. *It feels good to be taken care of, even for a little bit. This bed is very comfortable, but the room is little cool.*

David enters the room. "Everything okay? Here, I'll cover you with a woofy."

"What's a woofy? Oh, a little blanket."

"Yeah, that's what my little nephew called it. The name stuck," David says.

"You're tucking me in like a little kid."

"Yep."

"But I'm only taking a 15-minute nap."

"Shhhhh….." David closes the door quietly.

*   *   *

A few hours later, Susan comes out to the kitchen. "Gee, I'm sorry. I think I overslept. Guess I was more tired than I thought."

David's mother greets Susan with a smile and says, "Now it's time for supper. Why don't you stay the night and get a good start in the morning?"

The next morning, coming up from his basement room, David asks, "Do I smell bacon?"

"Yes, and French toast and fried eggs any way you want."

"I guess I was more tired than I thought," Susan adds. "Got up really early, started talking with your mom, then offered to make breakfast. I'm a professional, you know. How do you want your eggs? I can even do sunny side up!"

"These are the best eggs! Sorry Mom..." David adds. "Dad, I've got to go to Dodge to get that replacement bearing for the combine. We'll be cutting soon." He turns to Susan. "Susan! Come to Dodge City with me. You have to see our local historical tourist trap. I mean, since you've never been West, you really should see Dodge City. Come with me and you'll still have time to make it to Santa Fe today."

"Okay, but let's take my pickup. I owe you a tank of gas," Susan says. *His mom is so sweet, said she would clean up, and even thanked me for making breakfast and giving her a break.*

A few minutes later outside, Susan thinks, *He's looking at my truck like he really likes it. There's that smile again. He's starting to get in the passenger's side.*

"Would you like to drive? You can drive a stick shift?"

"Oh, come on."

"Just kidding, thanks for holding the door for me."

"My pleasure, ma'am. Usn' country boys know how."

"Oh, come on!" Susan says, smiling, *I think he is actually dancing for joy around to the driver's side. He has such a love of life in the moment.*

Running his hands over the fender, "Great truck! You want'a sell it?"

"No, I love my truck."

"We need a new pickup. Dad is so slow to buy any new equipment. Our old Chevy is almost twenty years old. I learned to drive in that truck."

"How old are you?"

"About twenty-nine. How old are you? Oops, sorry."

"It's okay. About twenty-nine …plus." *Susan thinks, I wonder what he's asking? Oh what the hell difference does it make what he thinks!"*

They drive North through miles and miles of ripening wheat.

"I'm trying to think what to say," David says. "Everything I think of sounds pretty stupid. Maybe I should stop the truck, back up a quarter mile, and start the conversation over."

"Oh god yes! If we could just do that… but I don't know how far back I would have to go."

"Yep, I guess we have to stay in the moment, then go on and do better the next time."

They ride along, each caught up in their own thoughts.

Susan scowls, "PHEWW! What's that's awful smell?"

"We are getting close to Dodge," David explains. "That's the stockyards where they feed cattle a very rich mixture of grain, chemicals, and who knows what. Gives the cattle diarrhea, their digestive system is not developed for grain," David says with distain. "We don't eat that meat. Some ranchers are raising grass fed beef and it's really good."

"Sounds gross," Susan responds. "I'm not a vegetarian, but I don't eat a lot of meat."

"Yeah, me too," David says. "Oh, there's Boot Hill. Sorry, we don't have time to stop. You'll just have come back to visit the museum and see the gun collection, the barb wire collection, the moth-eaten stuffed animals of the prairie, and—"

"That's okay, I'll pass."

David pulls into a parking space. "Here's the parts department for the combine. Want to come in and—"

"Sure, good to stretch my legs."

At the counter a young man asks, "Hi David. Who is this?"

"This is Susan, she's—"

"Good for you David! Glad to meet you, you take good care of David." The young man returns with the combine part. "When you start cutting?" he asks. "They've started just West of here. Hope you have some harvest help. Help's hard to come by. A lot of farmers are going to custom cutting, but look at that list! Not even enough custom cutters. See ya later, David, and you too Sue."

*   *   *

"This looks like a different way back," Susan says.

"Yeah, I want to show you something."

"I hope it's better than Boot Hill," she continues. "What did the parts man mean by taking care of you?"

David slows the truck. "Well, I've been wanting to tell you. I had a girlfriend in college, in Arkansas. We were very close, even sleeping together. We were going to get married the summer before my senior year, but—"

"What happened?" she asks. *I wonder if he's going to cry. No, just feeling deeply.*

"What was her name?"

He pauses, "Mary Lee. Her mother said she could not marry me and leave home. She said she needed Mary Lee at home to take care of her. I said she could bring her mother to live with us, but her mother didn't want to live in this god forsaken place that had no trees."

"She's right, there aren't many trees," Susan replies. "But that's pretty mean spirited of her to deny her daughter."

"So I transferred to K State, got my engineering degree, and here I am. Haven't had much success with dating." David looks at Susan with longing. "Guess I'm always comparing the date to Mary Lee. That's why the fellow in Dodge said what he did, he was glad to see me with someone."

Oh...Is the connection I feel for this man so obvious? Well, I do like him, but I want to get to Santa Fe, and soon!"

"Well, anyhow..." David looks ahead. "Oh my, look at that. Someone really hit the ditch. Must have been going pretty fast to tear out 50, 60 yards of ditch. Hope no one was hurt. You wouldn't think there would be any accidents out here with the roads so straight, seeing forever, and no traffic— HANG ON!"

"OH MY GOD!" Susan yells. "We're going to hit that cow!"

"Phew! Sure glad you've got good brakes!" says David. "Those Black Angus steers are hard to see. At night it's almost impossible, only the headlights reflecting in their eyes. Better stop and let Charles know he's got some stock out. There he is in the yard."

A young man, about David's age waves a greeting. "Hi ya David. Didn't recognize the new truck. Oh, you're the young woman in church that needed gas. My wife nagged me all the way home for not inviting you to dinner. Said you looked interesting. You still going to, where was it? Santa Fe?"

"I'm on my way," Susan says smiling, "as soon as we get back."

"Charles," David says, trying to mask his annoyance. "You got some stock out on the road. Black Angus are hard to see."

Charles, oblivious to David's mood says, "Thanks, I'll get on it right away. See ya. Have a good trip."

Driving on, David muses, "Yes, Charles is a good fellow, but way over his head with work. Can't seem to keep his fences in repair. He operates from a position of always being behind, and you know, he always is. I try and enjoy my work, I really do, and am thankful for the joy it brings me. It's hard to explain…"

"I understand, but I've never been able to put it into words," Susan says.

He seems so content with these long silences. He doesn't seem to have a need to fill up the space with his own voice.

*   *   *

"I want to show you something. That's my home."

"Nice, can we stop?"

David shakes his head, "No, don't have time if you're going to make it to Santa Fe. And, ah, I usually spend Sunday afternoon doing my housework, my laundry, etc. but ah, I was distracted yesterday. I'm not a slob, but…I do need to check the wheat, only take a moment."

David stops the truck and gets out.

He's walking out into the field totally surrounded by wheat, if he fell or knelt down, I would lose sight of him. This wheat is amazing! The colors, the sounds, the smells, the movement, and it totally surrounds and engulfs me. But in a wonderful, supportive, and even joyful way! He… I am at one with the wheat. Why do I feel like I'm taking part in an ancient ritual?

He sits down in the wheat on his knees, and takes her hand. "Come and sit beside me, I want to show you something."

"Hope it's better than Boot Hill."

"And maybe even better than a genuine Kansas windmill. Even though, you admit, that was pretty special." David reaches out. "I take one stock of wheat, break off the head, and rub it between the palms of my hands, I'm thrashing: separating the wheat grains from the chaff. And then a little puff to blow the chaff away, and here is the new crop. Taste it. Nothing in the world tastes like this."

She leans over, and with her tongue picks up the grains of wheat from the palm of David's hand.

He continues, "Feel the sun on your face, hear the wind whispering through the field, and smell. Too many odors to identify. Sometimes I wish I were a poet so I could describe all this. And now hearing you talk about your paintings, I wish I could capture all this with color."

He has done it again, transported me to another reality. But not really. I can see the roof of my truck, hear the train in the distance, and the jet contrails in the sky. But this is different, I'm different. Once again, I feel like I am a part of the wheat field, I am living. I am experiencing the—the colors. I'm dissolving. I'm the colors!

"Here, give me your hand," David says. "I take a single stalk of wheat and wrap it around your finger. See, some of the stalk is too brittle to wrap around, but some is still green enough to go all the way around. There, you have a golden ring." He leans back. "This is a very special time: the grains of wheat are ripe and ready, the chaff is loose, and it is time to harvest. In the old days, when the wheat was cut by hand with a scythe, the wheat was harvested before the grain was so loose." He paused, then continued. "But now, the combines need the wheat stalks to be dry and brittle enough to cut without jamming. Time stands still…We wait…The sun and the wind dry the stalks. We pray that there will be no windstorms to shake out the grains, or rain storms to soak the grains. It is a time of faith."

He's holding my hand. The golden ring is still on my—my ring finger.

Still holding her hand, David shifts around to face Susan. "We need to go, but first I want to say something. I have said things to you, a perfect stranger, that I have never said to anyone, some even to myself. You are the first real woman I have been able to talk with and not run it through a filter of a fantasy woman in Arkansas. I don't feel so lonely anymore."

We're kissing…I can't do this. I've got to go to Santa Fe. But oh, oh, oh! Wait. He is pulling me, almost roughly, to the truck. He's trying to break the spell.

"Stop, David," Susan says, pulling back. "Don't break the spell. You have said that you have an angel, a spirit guide that walks with you. But what I see is that you and your spirit are one…two aspects of the same being. Part of you is in this world of physical reality, but a part is in the spirit world. Both are very real and both are the same."

David stops, still holding her. Susan continues. "These two parts of you are working together to create. That's why you can go around saying that things always work out for you, and that you believe in and trust synchronicity. If you told anyone that you are both spirit and physical, you would probably get locked up in the loony bin. I have seen you slip into the other realm and I have followed you there. I became one with the colors and the sounds and the, the—you know. But I love you for it, and it has shown me how to approach my paintings. I thank you.

*   *   *

He's driving too fast. Maybe he just wants to get rid of me. He's pulling into the yard, but keeps going to the fuel tank.

"Oh David, you don't have to do that."

"Oh yeah. You go on to dinner, you have to eat before your long drive. I'll be there in a minute. I'm just taking the new bearing over to the combine."

Well, he may be both spirit and human, sometimes, but not now. He's a real human. I don't know if he is angry, sad, or what, but he has lost connection. I wish I could …

*   *   *

"Hi Dad, thanks for waiting dinner for us. Why so glum?"

Dad answers, "Bobby's dad called. He's okay, but totaled the car Saturday night. Ran off the road on his way back from Dodge. BROKE HIS ARM! Damn! Now we don't have a truck driver. Said he swerved to miss a steer, but I think maybe it was booze."

"Yea," David says. "We saw where he must have had the accident, and we almost hit a steer a quarter mile on down. It was Charles's Black Angus, very hard to see."

"So David," Dad asks. "What are we going to do? Maybe get custom cutters to—"

"No luck Dad. There's a list a mile long at the parts store. Maybe Mom could drive."

"No!" she says. "I can't do the scooping. I'm too old."

"Well, ah…" Susan speaks up. "I could drive, and I'm sure I could learn to use a scoop. That's a kind of shovel, right? I've scooped snow in the East. Is wheat that much harder?"

"But Susan, what about Santa Fe?" David asks.

"So, how long is harvest? A few weeks. And then I'm on to Santa Fe. You do pay, right?'

"And room and board. Mom is a great cook!" David jumps up. "Dad, we've got to get moving. We'll be cutting tomorrow or the next day. Can you get on replacing the bearing?"

"Susan, unpack your truck and move into the guest room. Mom will show you everything. I'll get the wheat truck out and show you how to drive a real stick shift truck. Yeah. Dual speed transmission with a granny, and a two-speed differential. And a power take off to run the dump. Whooowe!"

He's got his spirit back! Things seem to work out for him.

David brings the large dump truck with a twenty-foot bed up to the house. "All moved in? Let's take a drive into town. I'll show you how to dump the grain at the elevator."

Susan drives for a few minutes getting used to the multiple gears and the clutch.

David is smiling. "You're a natural driving this truck, but remember, with a load on it's going to drive very differently. Wheat is heavy."

After the driving lesson, and the practice run at the elevator, Susan returns to the farm and brings the truck alongside the fuel tank.

David, obviously delighted, says. "You were great! I'm so glad you're staying to help. We'll turn in pretty early after supper. May be cutting—"

Susan jumps out of the truck and slams the door. "I'm so excited. Never thought I would be driving a truck and actually working at harvest."

They walk together back to the house. He says, "After supper, I want to show you something."

"Better than a whole field of wheat almost ready?"

David stops and takes her hand. "Maybe not better, but bigger, and total color. You'll love it."

Everyone is quiet at supper. I guess everyone is thinking about harvest. Maybe this is the way they pray for good weather."

After supper, they go out to the barn, holding hands.

David stops, stalling for time. Then on around behind the barn.

Susan lets out a gasp. "Oh! Look at that! I have never seen a sunset like this…The whole sky is filled with color…to the horizon, whichever direction you look. The sun is just above the ends of the earth out west." Susan continues to marvel. "And the sun light across the wheat fields, unbelievable color! Oh, look behind us, the eastern sky is also full of color." She takes his hand. "Oh David, thank you!" She pauses. "You see beauty in everything, every moment. You are so aware of the world around you. Do you ever miss anything?"

"Sometimes, when I'm not focused," David answers, "But then, sometimes the beauty is so… so intense. It's sometimes, well, almost excruciating! And we get a new show every day. Better turn in early…big day tomorrow."

*　*　*

Susan, awakes, realizes she has to pee. *It's so dark in here. That toilet makes so much noise, I'll just go outside. UMMMMMM smells good out here. I can smell the wheat, it feels pregnant.* "Oh David! I didn't see you. I—"

"Had to pee too? Why didn't you use the facilities in the house? I'm very happy you came outside, I wanted to show you the night sky. I was thinking how I could describe this to you, no glow of city lights, and here on the high prairie, at about 2,500 feet. The stars are so close, and so many of them. You can actually see the Milky Way."

Susan lifts her face to the skies. *He's taking me to another place again. I have never seen the night sky so, so, …huge. I'm getting that same feeling of being at one with the whole world around me. This is the feeling I'm looking for when I paint. I kinda dissolve, no… merge into the whole.*

"Pretty wonderful, isn't it?"

He's taking me in his arms, I can feel his body through my t-shirt and panties. She presses herself into him. *Even though it's dark, I can tell all he has on are his shorts. Why is he stopping? Maybe he's not ready, sure feels like he's ready, maybe he doesn't want to get too involved, but then why would he kiss me twice in one day?*

*   *   *

It's just getting light.

David's voice echoes through the house, "Come on everybody! TODAY'S THE DAY!"

Breakfast is eaten in a hurry and in silence.

Susan follows the men from the trucks into the field, observing. The machinery is lined up behind them, fueled and ready to start. The ritual begins: a short walk into the wheat, drop to our knees, break off a head of wheat, thrash it between our palms, and taste the grains. Then the wrapping of the straw around the finger…the straw splinters, will not wrap.

"LET'S DO IT," David shouts! Everyone smiles in agreement.

After a few rounds of cutting, the combine unloads into the truck Susan's driving. When the truck is full, she drives the load of wheat to the grain elevator in town. Dumping the load, scooping out the corners of the truck bed. Back to the field, take on another load of wheat.

David, obviously very happy, says, "This is a good year."

Mom brings dinner to the field. The harvest crew eats quickly.

I drive more trips to town. A short break for ice tea.
We continue cutting after dark. I'm getting tired.
The grain elevator in town stays open late.

Suddenly, the cutter bar on the combine starts to bang bang bang. The evening dew has set in, and the straw is too tough to cut. The combines are lined up at the edge of the field, ready for servicing in the morning.

I drive the pickup back to the house with David's dad. I offered to let him drive, but he says he is too tired.

Susan takes a quick shower and returns to her room to dress. She hears the voices of the men through the heat vent as they shower in the basement next to the furnace. The shower stops and she hears David's dad say, "—and she's a good worker. Glad she came by."

Susan smiles knowing that David would be thinking, "No accident."

The harvest crew take a quick supper of white bread, lunch meat, packaged cheese, mustard, mayonnaise, a lettuce leaf, and a glass of milk. There is no talking, everyone is too tired.

The next morning, which comes way too early, everyone is up at first light. A hearty breakfast, then out to the field to service the combines. Susan pumps gas into the fuel tanks from barrels in the old pick up. The men pump grease into every bearing in the two combines. Every few minutes they all go through the ritual of testing the wheat stalks for dryness. Then, "LET'S DO IT!"

And harvest starts again.

I lose track of the days. After a while, we move the operation to the fields in the north, near David's home. He and I move into his home, to be closer to the fields and not have to drive back at night when we're tired. I get the guest room. I make breakfast. Kinda fun being domestic again. No conflict except who showers first. We work it out.

*   *   *

Harvest is over.

"Hey Susan, want to ride the last rounds with me?"

She climbs up the steep ladder and into the combine cab. "It's so crowded up here. Where do I sit?"

"On my lap, just don't touch any levers, buttons, or pedals." David starts cutting the last round. Even in the enclosed cab, the sound of the machine is almost deafening.

Susan feels the physical intimacy being so close to David, but she's thinking. *It's a very different perspective up here, about eight feet. What was once great fields of wheat moving and swaying in the breezes, is now dry stubble as far as the eye can see. All is dry, and dead, and empty. I feel an urge to get away.*

David says, "That's it… harvest is over. You take the truck back. I'll follow with a combine. It feels kind of empty doesn't it?" David climbs down after Susan. He pauses, almost seeming at a loss as to what to do next. The work, the long hours, the daily exhaustion is now over.

Finally David speaks, "I always feel a little let down after harvest. That's why I like to take a vacation, a little trip. A few years ago, I went to Santa Fe feeling pretty rung out. I learned to meditate, and that really helped. Saw an ad for a yoga class. Didn't like the yoga much, but did like the meditations. Been doing it ever since. Well, see you at the house." David climbs back on the combine and drives away, leaving Susan with the truck and her thoughts.

Damn, I'm tired! But harvest is done. Maybe it is just the letdown of being finished. Took longer than I expected because as soon as we finished our harvest, we got another job. Charles asked us to help out. His combine broke down completely. He tried to get a custom cutter to finish harvest, but they were all booked.

David said we would do it for the same price, and that included me! What am I doing saying, we? So, I made a little more money for Santa Fe. I'm ready for a shower, then a nap before supper.

As Susan enters the house, David greets her, "It's good to get home early, before sunset. I've been meaning to give you something, but it has always been too dark."

Susan stops on her way to the shower. He is reaching for something at his window of Cobalt glass, it must be special.

"This is a piece of polished Amber. I found it in Santa Fe."

"Amber?"

"Yeah, ancient fossilized tree resin. I picked this one for the color, didn't need the ones that have insects trapped inside. You have been talking about capturing the color of the wheat fields. Well, 'Amber waves of grain'.… It's for you."

Susan takes the amber and holds it up to the light. "Oh my god! You are so right! On the color wheel, amber is between metallic gold and earthy orange. But the real amber is a multitude of colors; gold, orange, brown, some red copper, and even some green. All of them translucent and in different intensities. It is so beautiful! I wonder if I could grind up amber to make a paint color. You know, the intense blue gowns of the Medieval Madonnas were ground up Lapis stone."

"You can grind up this if you want," David says, "But there is a gem shop in Santa Fe which has small pieces of amber."

"Oh David, I would never destroy this, it's so beautiful!"

"I have always liked amber," David says, "I like the color, the feel and I like the sound of the word. AMMMMmmber. Like: "I AM." I have thought, if I ever have a daughter that I would name her Amber… Well, enough of this. I'm off to take a shower."

"No David, I'm on my way to the shower now.

"Wait! I gotta shower first. I'm so dusty and smelly…"

"No, me first, I've got chaff all over, even in my undies. And I itch."

David produces a coin, "Let's flip for it… call."

"Heads…"

"Tails…"

"David, how did you do that? It landed on edge!"

With a grin, David says, "Guess we'll have to shower together."

*   *   *

"Oh, David, oh, oh …

*   *   *

That was so intense! Wonder if he's awake.

David opens his eyes, sensing that Susan is awake. "That was really wonderful and… I just don't have the words…"

"Me too…"

David crawls out of bed and slips into a pair of sweatpants. "You hungry? I think we missed supper. I'll heat up a frozen pizza. Do you want a beer?"

"I can't move. Let's eat in bed."

"Mmmmmmmmm…"

"I can't understand your mumble."

Susan looks over at David. "This is the best pizza ever. David, why didn't you make love to me weeks ago? Did you not want to?"

David reaches over to caress her. "I've wanted to make love with you ever since I saw you that first time in church."

"Then why not?"

"I didn't want to come on too fast or too…you know. Then, I realized if we made love I would fall in love, and if you went to Santa Fe—"

"I'm going tomorrow morning."

"—that I would have a broken heart."

"So what changed your mind or convictions?"

"That's a no brainer…I took one look at you in the shower and I figured it was worth the gamble."

"Thanks, David! So, who won?"

"Don't know. You haven't left yet."

"Are you trying to keep me here?"

"No, you have to follow your own bliss and that seems to be painting in Santa Fe. If I kept you here, someday you would resent me for it."

"Thank you. I love you for your understanding and support."

Susan slips under the sheets. "I'm so tired. Do you mind if I stay here in your bed and not go to the guest room?"

Early the next morning, Susan gently closes the door of her pickup and heads west towards Santa Fe. The thoughts in her mind come almost too fast. *I love first light and the open road before me. I'm so excited, on my way at last. Maybe it was mean of me to slip out before David woke up, but I think neither of us wanted the "goodbyes." Damn, I'm starting to feel that old glum again. Sun is coming up behind me and glaring in my mirrors. I hear David saying: look at the positive, look at the beauty, feel the joy in the moment. I did enjoy the first light, but then I started to feel glum and the glare was not so enjoyable. Thinking about my time with the harvest, and then about my time with David… I feel that I have a little bit of David in me. OH NO! Not that little bit…I mean a little bit of his spirit. He did offer to use protection, but I said I was about to get my period, and it was OK. I mean, can two people have the same spirit? It's like I keep hearing his voice in my head.*

"Follow your bliss, and go to Santa Fe."

"I believe in synchronicity, look for it. Let it happen."

"Look for the beauty in everything, and enjoy."

With the extra money made working the harvest Susan knows she will not have to look for a job first thing, but can start painting again. It's been too long.

I'm so filled with anticipation of what's coming next. I hope I can believe, as does David, that everything always works out. I can hardly wait to open my paints. I tried to paint during the harvest; the colors, the sounds, the dust and chaff, and even the sweaty smell of the men working. I guess I also smelled. I haven't worked so hard since, well, ever.

I bet he's going to Dodge to buy a new pickup. I wonder what color it will be? Maybe he will let me paint it for him. I think I would paint it the colors of ripening wheat, like amber.

*   *   *

David drives to his folk's place for breakfast thinking I sure like this new pickup. Hard to get Dad to buy new equipment, but we did have a good harvest. I hope after breakfast I can get Dad to talk more about what he wants to do with the farm. We could sell out, they could move to town. But Dad would go stir crazy not having anything to do. I could take an engineering job, maybe with renewable energy. David pauses. Maybe in Santa Fe. What am I thinking? Wonder how's Susan? Haven't heard from her for a few weeks. At first she was writing all about her apartment, taking painting classes at the O'Keefe Museum, a new job, and new friends. She seemed so happy, wonder if she is OK. I'm a farmer, I don't think I could work for a paycheck.

His thoughts turn to a dream he had about Mary Lee, and the fire he built the next day where he burned all her photos. After throwing the ashes in the air she was gone, making room for a new relationship.

Wonder if I were to get married if Dad would give me the farm? The other kids are both set up in business and doing well. They want nothing to do with the farm. I think I'll call Susan after breakfast.

As he pulls into the yard, his mom calls out. "Susan's on the line. Said she called you at home, but no answer so called here. She sounds troubled."

He jumps out of the truck and runs to the house, picking up the phone in the kitchen. "Hi Susan, you OK?"

"Hi David, just fine… I guess. What are you doing?"

"I'm driving my new pick up when I can get it away from Dad. What's up? You sure you're OK?"

"Oh David, I've gotten myself into a bit of a situation and I don't know what to do, and I thought if I could just talk with you it would help me to…you know…"

"Sure, what's going on? Are you sure you're OK? Haven't wrecked your pickup?"

"No, no, no, I just…I can't talk about it on the phone with your mother right there and…I want to see you in person, but I don't think I can drive all that way—"

Before she finishes, David says, "I'm coming. I'll get some breakfast and I'll be there in nine hours. Don't go away!"

"Mom, I'm going to see Susan, she needs me. Tell Dad I'll be back before planting. And can you pack me a lunch?"

David runs downstairs to his old bedroom, packs a bag with clean clothes, eats a quick breakfast, grabs his lunch, and is on the road.

Hope she is alright. Glad I have a good truck to drive. Wonder what's going on? Maybe I'll look into the job market in that area. I don't know…I don't think I could work for a weekly paycheck. Maybe, we… I don't think she would like living on the prairie. Just about have to be born to it. Wish there was a way to try out marriage for a year, if it doesn't work there's no judgment. Wouldn't work in my community. Kansas has a lot of beauty, but also a lot of death and dying. But then there's new life happening all the time. I guess that's what farming is all about, nurturing new life. I wonder if she's pregnant?

David lifts his eyes to the distance. Oh, there's the mountains on the horizon. I remember the first time I saw them. I was about eight, went to see my aunt. I had heard so much about the majestic mountains. I was so disappointed, the mountains were just little blue bumps on the horizon. It was dark before we got to Colorado Springs. The next morning I awoke with mountains all around me. Never saw anything like it on the flat prairie! I wonder what Susan grew up with, and now with such a contrast between the prairie and the mountains. She seems to adapt pretty well, sees things in depth that I only see on the surface. I wonder what she sees in me? Maybe she's pregnant. Wonder what she's going to do. And maybe she's not. But I did see that little blue light around us after we made love.

David focuses on the driving for a few miles, then thinks. I do want to father a child, but maybe this is not the right time. Maybe it was a little being wanting to join in, or maybe it was the special-ness of the lovemaking, or both.

* * *

Susan is overjoyed to see David, "Thank you for coming. Yes, yes, hold me for a minute."

"Are you sure you're OK? You're crying!"

"Just relieved, happy, thankful, and, and—"

"Let's sit down, my legs are a little wobbly from driving. So, what's up? Talk to me."

Susan looks down, then up at David.

"It's... I'm... it's not your fault... it's my responsibility. I'm pregnant! Oh God, what do I do?"

"Have you thought through the options?"

With a shudder, Susan forces a response. "Abortion, full-term and then adoption, or single motherhood. All seem overwhelming. What should I do? I usually can make up my mind about things, but I'm all confused on this."

David reaches out and gently pulls her to his lap.

"If everything were all OK, would you want a child?"

Susan lays her head on his shoulder; he places his hand on her belly.

"Yes, yes, I'm over thirty and wonder when, if ever."

With gentle conviction, David says, "How about we raise this new little visitor... together."

BING

This year they planted a short variety of wheat, only 18 or 20 inches tall. This requires the cutter bar on the front of the combine harvester to be run much lower, very close to the ground. I am working on my uncle's farm in western Kansas, on the prairie south of Dodge City. Today is the second day of harvest. Yesterday was a good day. The new, shorter variety is paying off. As hoped, there is less energy going into the stems and more into the grain head. We're getting more than twenty bushels of wheat to the acre.

It is still dark when we come up for breakfast. As usual, breakfast is scrambled eggs, bacon, oatmeal cooked with raisins and cinnamon, served with real cream, buttered toast, and glasses of milk. Only my cousin has coffee, a habit he learned in college.

After breakfast, the leftover food is scraped into the dog's bowl. We grab our jackets and pile into the pickup. I ride in the back with the hired hand, the large drum of gasoline, the grease guns, various tools, and the dog.

The morning is cool. As the sun gets a little higher the morning dew burns off and we can start harvest. At the field the men stand around, waiting, each quietly containing his own excitement or restlessness. We are: my uncle, my cousin David, a hired hand, and myself. The dog is not even trying to contain his excitement; running, bouncing through the wheat looking for a rabbit, maybe one still asleep in the morning cool. When he comes back to the group, no one wants to pet him. His short, black fur is glossy wet from the dew. I'm just a kid, fifteen years old, well, fourteen and 3/4, and a truck driver. This is the first summer that I'm actually on the payroll.

The machinery is ready. The combines are fueled and greased. The trucks are lined up. I'm given the old '38 Chevy to drive. It has classic bullet headlights on top of the front fenders, the rest of the truck is pretty much rusted out. It is older than me. The exhaust system has fallen away years ago and been replaced by a section of two-inch water pipe. Very loud, but perfect for a teenager. The sun is up, the dew is burned off, the men throw their jackets in the back of the pickup. It is time to start harvest.

My job is to watch the combines as they circle the field, and to meet them when they need to off-load the grain into my truck. I drive along beside the moving combine positioning my truck under the off-load spout. When my truck is full, after three or four loads, I drive to the grain elevator in town to have the wheat weighed and dumped.

The women have just arrived with dinner, the hearty mid-day meal. We pull into the field together. The aroma, when I open the car's trunk, increases my hunger. As usual, dinner is a rich beef stew served in the electric skillets with their glass lids that the stew was cooked in. In addition, there are canned pears floating in green Jello, ice tea, and pumpkin pie still warm from the oven. My cousin, just finishing a round, is ready to stop for dinner. To keep the harvest going, I will operate the combine while he eats. My aunt gives me a slice of pie to hold me over until it is my time to eat.

David stops the combine, but leaves it running. He sees the wide grin on my face. He knows, being just out of his teens, the indescribable joy for a kid, of driving a huge piece of machinery, as large as a small house. He shouts out above the roar of the engine, "Keep the cutter bar low enough, but not down in the dirt. Remember, we're harvesting, not plowing!"

This is not the only thing I have to keep in mind. The engine speed and the thrashing drum speed are preset. But the volume of wheat fed into the thrashing drum is determined by how fast the combine travels over the ground. The only way to judge the speed is by the pitch of the howling sound from the thrashing drum. So the forward speed is very important, as is controlling the steering to keep the combine cutting a full swath next to the previously cut wheat. My left hand rests on the steering wheel, grasping a steering ball. The height of the cutting bar is constantly adjusted by a lever at my right hand. The forward speed controlled by another lever at the right. At my feet, a left and right brake help in tight turns. Driving a combine is very exciting, very demanding, very tiring, and most of all, very enjoyable. I finish my round. David has finished his dinner, and is ready to take over. As he drives away, the dog follows.

I eat quickly, return to my truck, take on some off-loads, and watch. My cousin stops his combine on the other side of the field, about a half mile away. He must have had a breakdown. I drive around the field and stop next to the combine under the off loading spout. Once out of the cab, the only sound is the whispering of the wind in the dry wheat and the

PING

PING...

......PING

of the hot engine cooling down. David, his shirt covered with blood, is on his knees. I think he is seriously injured, but he is scooping the soft prairie soil into a pile. I see a tuft of black fur, a tail, sticking out from under the pile of soil. I kneel beside David and he looks up. His dusty face lined with the muddy streaks of tears.

"He was chasing a jack rabbit down a furrow," David says. "The rabbit went under— the combine, but—he— I got the machine stopped before he was pulled up into the thrashing drum, but I had to pull him out." David's voice breaks. "All four paws were gone. I laid him on the ground. He looked...up at me and he said,"

I can't stand up. Help me...

"As he looked at me, I helped him," David said, his voice trailing off, "the only way I could. I smashed his skull with a heavy wrench."

David lies down with his arms around the mound, his face buried in the warm prairie. His body jerking as he sobs deep, gut-wrenching moans.

He stands up, slaps the dust off his jeans, starts the combine, off-loads what wheat he has in the bin, and continues around the field. My load is full, so I drive to the grain elevator in town by the back country roads. My eyes fill with tears, the loud exhaust muffles my sobs.

Tonight, as usual, supper is white bread, lunch meat, square slices of American cheese, mustard, mayonnaise, a few lettuce leaves, and a glass of milk. As usual, there is little conversation between us men, tired from a long day's harvest work.

Everyone knows, but no one speaks.

Bing is gone.

THE WAVE

We are in a typhoon. Between Honolulu and Yokohama, Japan. Sailing aboard the SS *President Cleveland*.

Our cabin is very small for a family of four, with two bunk beds, room for only one to dress at a time. The rolling of the ship is making me nauseated. I'm going up to the lounge. My folks remind me to stay inside and not go out on deck.

The lounge is in the front of this passenger/freighter ship, the second deck down from the top. The lifeboats are just outside. Full windows on three sides give a panoramic view of the ocean. Stepping into the back of the lounge from the hallway, I am confronted by a different world.

First, there is an eight-inch rise at the threshold of the room. This is to keep any sea water that might get in from draining into the hallway and inner parts the ship.

Second, every chair, table, and plant stand has been lashed with heavy ropes to sturdy railings along the walls.

Third, a group of Pentecostal missionaries are huddled together at the far end of the room, singing.

Nearer, my God, to Thee
Nearer to Thee
The sun gone down
Darkness be over me
My rest a stone
angels to beckon me
Nearer, my God, to Thee

The lounge, so high above the water, offers a commanding view of the surrounding ocean. We were told that we would be sailing into a storm, that there would be rough seas, and to stay off the open decks. No one said the word "typhoon."

Nearer, My God, to Thee

The sea stretches out beyond us, large waves one after another. The ship meets each wave slightly to the right of its center. The ship drives up the face of the wave, and because of the slope, heels to the right.

Cresting the top of the wave, the bow is so high the view of the ocean ahead is blocked. The ship comes crashing down the back side of the wave, solid green water floods over the bow and fore deck, spray hitting the windows. The wave passes under the ship, the twin propellers come close to the surface of the water and cavitate sucking air down around the mighty blades. The drive engines howl. The props plunge again, deep in the sea, causing the ship to shudder as the spinning blades bite.

Nearer, My God, to Thee

A chair breaks loose from its lashings and skids across the room, crashing into stacks of furniture. The ship rolls and the chair slides back across the room. No one tries to capture it.

Wave after wave comes, and is met. Our ship drives forward, up with a roll and over the top, plunging into the next to repeat the sequence. The rolling and plunging movement of the ship is predictable. Even the hymn singers are less intense.

From the windows, the oncoming waves can be seen stretching to the horizon. Out there, perhaps a mile or so ahead, appears a mountain. It doesn't even look like a wave it is so tall, so huge. The singers do not see it coming. There is no place to hide. I tighten my grip on the railing near the door. My first thought is, if the windows break, will the eight-inch threshold at the door keep the sea water from getting inside the ship?

We meet the wave. The ship starts its climb up the face of the mountain. The wave is so high I can't see the top through the lounge windows. The ship seems to be standing on end. A table breaks loose and slides over the floor, crashing into the wall near me. One of the hymn singers loses his grip and glides across the floor sprawled.

What started out as a verse of "Nearer, My God"...becomes a terrifying scream. The singers are no longer singing, they are screaming and crying.

I wonder where their faith is?

We continue to climb up the wave, and the ship starts its roll to the right. The ship has rolled on each wave before, but I have always been able to see the sky through the right-side windows. Now, all I see down through the glass is the surface of the sea. We are heeling over so far that solid green sea water is boiling up over the railing and deck on the right side. How much farther can we roll? People are sliding across the floor.

Nearer, My God, to Thee

We make it over the top. The propellors, having struggled so powerfully to keep the ship moving forward up the wave, are now above the surface in the air, their rpm spinning out of control, screaming a high-pitched howl. Then, back into the sea, taking a mighty bite in the water, causing the ship to shudder as if breaking loose from a death grip.

Racing down the back side of this huge wave, the bow plunges deep into the next wave. Solid green water comes over the bow and keeps coming. The ship plunges deeper and deeper. Water washes over the fore deck and keeps coming. The whole front of the ship is underwater. The green sea slams against the lounge windows. This is not spray. This is ocean. These windows are three decks above the main deck. The buoyancy of the ship takes control and with violent shaking throws off the heavy sea water.

Nearer, My God, to Thee

Ten years later, I'm aboard the SS *President Wilson*, the sister ship of the SS *President Cleveland*, planning on back-packing through Southeast Asia. I strike up a conversation with a young ship's officer, the Purser. I mention that I was on the west bound 1949 Christmas cruise of the SS *President Cleveland*.

The officer stumbles a little and reaches out to grab a handrail. "Tell me about it," he struggles to say. "All of us who are a part of American President Line company have heard the stories. But never firsthand from a passenger."

Before I can tell my story, the Purser tells me the facts as he knew them. The SS *President Cleveland* was built for the war effort, with the most advanced designs in steam/electric drive, and a new hull design. Because it was a new design, the hull had to be tested. With added ballast and cables, the hull was pulled over on its side to test for stability in a roll. The test went to 43 degrees. Any more than 45 degrees, the naval architects had calculated, the ship would continue its roll, ending up on its side or sinking. This test was, of course, not an actual sea trial, nor with cargo that might shift in a roll.

"The voyage you were on," he said, "the ship rolled 43 degrees to starboard. The most any ship had ever rolled and survived."

He releases his grip on the railing and takes my hand. We look at each other. In that look there is knowing between us. Knowing the power of the sea. Knowing the power of life and death.

Since that time I have begun to understand these things. By nineteen, I'm on my way, exploring my spirituality, studying, meditating, and questioning my religious upbringing. I have experienced joy so great that words can't express the fullness of the emotion. Other times I have sought answers to unanswerable questions about my personal relationship with the Divine, sometimes confronting death head-on.

It has been an exciting adventure for a lifetime.

Nearer, My God, to Thee

The SS *President Cleveland.*
The lounge is behind the lifeboats

BROKEN SHIP

"This vessel is going to the ship-breakers," says the maître d'. "You know, the scrap yard. As soon as we arrive in Marseille, the end."

"But why can't we have clean table linen?" asks my dad.

"Because everything is old, not working," answers the maître d'. "And now it's the laundry machines." He pauses, and adds, "This ship is falling apart."

We eat on dirty table linen for the next few days. Little did we know, that would be the least of it.

It was 1953. We, my parents, sister, and myself, were on our way home from the Philippine Islands. Our family had spent the last four years in Manila. My parents, both educators, worked in schools and hospitals. It was now time to continue our circumnavigating the world back to the USA. We were aboard the MV *Felix Russell*, a French passenger/cargo ship bound for Marseille.

We had sailed west in 1949, heading to Manila from San Francisco, aboard the SS *President Cleveland*. On our way to the Philippines our ship stopped in Yokohama, Japan. We saw no visible signs of war there. Only block after block of cleared and leveled lots.

We arrived in Manila, the "Pearl of the Orient," just after the war ended. Our ship weaved its way between the sunken wrecks in the harbor, my first images of the horrors of war. I was nine years old. I knew ships are meant to be floating, not turned upside down, or on their sides. Many of the ships had blast holes in their hulls, with their steel plates peeled back, allowing the waters of the shallow harbor to flow in and out. We docked at a pile of rubble, what was left of the pier and its buildings. Climbing around mounds of broken concrete and steel, we went into the city to our new life. Manila was one huge war zone of bombed out buildings, twisted steel structures, and people with missing legs, barely able to walk.

Pock marks covered the face of my school building, holes left by the spray of machine gun fire. And in my classroom, some of my fellow students were a head shorter than the rest of us, due to serious malnutrition while detained in concentration camps during the war. Sometimes, during quiet study period, the sounds of gut-wrenching sobs came from these students. Looking across the room, one could see them, face down on their desks, bodies shaking with their cries. No wonder, with the memories those kids held. Their stories, though seldom told, were horrific. A friend, another child, killed in front of them by repeated blows and hacks of a shovel. Others told stories so painful and gruesome I can't bring myself to retell them here.

So, at nine years of age, I experienced war. Not the John Wayne heroes of battle, but the dirty, gritty aftermath of war; broken minds, broken bodies, broken buildings, and broken ships, experiences which affected my life decisions far into the future.

On our way home, the MV *Felix Russell* stops in the noisy, bustling city of Hong Kong. There is tension in the air. Communist China is just a short distance inland from the shoreline which faces the British controlled island holding the city.

The next port of call is Saigon. Our ship ties to the quay along the bank of the Mekong River, at the foot of a wide boulevard leading back into the city. We are to depart early the next morning. The city is beautiful, but quiet. An eerie quiet, a quiet that I had not experienced in any of the other cities I had already visited in the Far East.

We are up early and waiting on deck. And waiting. All the ship's officers are dressed in their best uniforms. They too are waiting, smoking, and pacing. An announcement blares out of the loud-speakers. As usual, it is only in French. We ask a fellow passenger what they said.

"It is nothing," he replies.

The faint sounds of a military band drift to us. As the band turns down the boulevard towards our ship, we hear the notes of "La Marseillaise," the French national anthem. The band marches up to the ship and spreads out on the dock below facing us. Behind them there are about 200 foot soldiers, some in fine uniforms, others in ragged regalia, and more than a few walking with crutches. The band continues to play rousing military music. The soldiers board the ship in single file by the forward gang plank. It is easy to see how dilapidated and bent many of them are, the once proud and powerful French Foreign Legion. Their officers direct them to climb down ladders through the open cargo hatches into the space below.

From the promenade deck above I can see down the ladders into the cargo hold where rough bunks, six beds high have been constructed. As they arrive, each soldier claims a bunk. I can't imagine what it would be like down there, no sunlight, bad air, and men jammed together. But, at least, they're going home after fighting in the jungles of Vietnam, Laos, and Cambodia. The officers come aboard and join the passengers on the deck above, where each is assigned to a stateroom, four or six to a room. The band stops playing. They are the last to board.

The gang plank is stowed, the hatch covers are placed and bolted down tight. The horn gives a long blast, signaling that the ship is about to back into the traffic lanes of the river. There are no other ships in sight. The blast seems to last longer than is necessary.

Perhaps it is a farewell. The MV *Felix Russell* has just picked up the last of the French Foreign Legion from French Indochina, now called Vietnam, thus ending almost 100 years of colonial occupation.

The steamship company, Messageries Maritimes, operators of the MV *Felix Russell*, are at the end of their Far East shipping service. Even though they made other ports of call in Asia, the lucrative Vietnam connection is no more.

Transporting the last of the French Foreign Legion home will be their final shipment of cargo and passengers.

We are told to stay off the open decks, the Communists might fire on the departing ship.

I stand behind a steel lifeboat support on the open deck. Looking across the vast Mekong delta on our way back to the sea, I wonder what's next for this beautiful country. I hope it will not be the site of military conflict, leaving the country in a pile of rubble.

Our next port of call is Singapore. There's no cargo to load or off-load. We take on a few new passengers, mostly French business-men and their families who are afraid of what's going to happen in Southeast Asia with the Communist takeover of Vietnam. A young couple comes aboard and joins us for meals at our table for six. They speak English. He is Australian, a freelance writer who loves to drink. She is a Filipina who loves to dance and becomes very popular with the French officers.

Departing Singapore, our ship backs around in the narrow, shallow harbor. And runs aground on a mud bank. One of the blades of the three-bladed twin propellors is bent. Not too serious, the ship can still move under power. But the ship shakes, and shakes, and shakes. The shaking is so bad that a full water glass will splash its contents onto the table.

It's hot in the Indian Ocean. It must be miserable for the soldiers down in the cargo hold. They are allowed out on deck, in small groups, for thirty minutes, twice a day. For them, the only good thing is that they're going home. Sometimes, when the hatch cover is moved enough to let a small group out on deck, the smell of unwashed bodies reaches our deck above. We, as passengers, are not allowed to visit the soldiers on the deck below.

The ship stops in Ceylon. We are ecstatic. We can go ashore, away from the constant shaking.

At sea again, we realize that we have slowed down, and maybe the shaking is less. The ship is now traveling at eleven knots, not the eighteen knots we had made before.

"Why have we slowed down so much?" my dad asks an officer.

"The ship is shaking itself to death," says the officer. "Already, some of the rivets in the steel plates of the hull have popped out. We have pumps running full-time."

The MV *Felix Russell* was built for the Far East trade, with the latest innovations. She had two huge diesel engines, not the traditional steam. Thus, MV (motor vessel) not SS (steam ship) in her name. She was converted for the war effort in WW I and reconverted after the war back to a passenger/cargo vessel. During WW II, she was once again a vital part of the war. Now she's on her way home and the ship-breakers for dismantling. Everything is breaking down. Even the crew are going to retire once we arrive in Marseille. Many of them have worked on this ship their whole adult life. The Far East trade with Vietnam is over. The new world-wide airline passenger service has almost ended the passenger ship business. The increased use of cargo containers requires a totally different design for ships. With the end in sight, why clean?

Increasing numbers of cockroaches become our dinner companions.

The ship is running out of drinking water. We're told not to drink out of the cold water tap in the bathroom. It has been diluted with sea water to make it go farther. With so many passengers return-ing home, all the soldiers in the cargo hold, and the hot weather, potable water has become a major issue.

There is drinking water aboard, bottles of French mineral water. But they cost about the same as a bottle of French wine. Each night, two bottles of wine come with dinner, one red and one white. My parents do not drink, and neither does the young couple sitting with us. They prefer a mixed drink which they bring down from the bar. The wine is returned after dinner unopened.

My dad asks the maître d', "Please bring us two bottles of water."

"Of course, sir, still or with gas?"

"One of each."

"I will put the tab on your bar bill," says the maître d'.

"No. Water instead of wine."

"Oh, I am so sorry. I can't do that."

"I've seen you," says my dad, "selling crates of wine at each port. That's my wine you're selling, because I don't drink it."

"I'm sorry," says the maître d'. "I can't make the exchange."

"Okay," says my dad. "The wine is mine. I will do with it what I want."

"Of course, sir."

"If there is no mineral water on the table tonight," says my dad, "I will open the port hole by our table and throw the wine bottles out to sea."

"Oh, no sir, you can't do that."

"Yes, I can," he says.

That night there are two bottles of wine on the table as usual. Our dining companion, the Australian writer, urges my dad to open the porthole and do it. He senses a story.

My dad stands up, struggles to open the corroded porthole. Once the port is open, he turns to reach for a bottle of wine. Just as his hand is about to close on the neck of the wine bottle, a bottle of mineral water is slipped into his grip. Another bottle of water is set on the table and the two bottles of wine disappear.

We have two bottles of French mineral water on our table each evening for the remainder of the trip.

My dad has shown me how to face conflict head on, with a creative solution, and not be afraid to act. This lesson has stayed with me.

We stop in Djibouti, French Somalia, to take on potable water. This was not a regular port of call for the ship, there usually wasn't enough trade in this poor country to justify a stop. After we've departed we find out that the tanker barge that delivered our drinking water had been used to haul diesel fuel.

The water is awful.

In Egypt, every street in Cairo is protected by at least two uniformed soldiers armed with rifles. King Farouk has been dethroned by a military coup. In my imagination, I'm trying to integrate the timelessness of the Pyramids and the Sphinx, with the present time of political/military unrest. This appears to be a condition of the whole earth. I am beginning to ponder my place in the world. It's a big question for a thirteen-year-old.

The answers come to me slowly, but powerfully in the years to come.

As we sail across the Mediterranean Sea on our way to Marseille, more things on the ship stop working. Spills in the dining room are not cleaned up. Doors will not open easily, or they will not stay closed. And on and on.

We head into a storm and the waves build. The ship rolls. Strange sounds come from somewhere in the vessel. Loud bangs, followed by terrifying groans. Is this the death rattle of a dying ship? The engines have slowed down. Less shaking, less vibration. Maybe the rivets in the hull plates will hold for a few more days.

Suction hoses snake through open hatch covers down into the cargo hold where the soldiers bunk. Water pumps on deck are running full on. The discharge flows across the deck and over the side through the scuppers.

I wonder how deep the water has gotten in the hold. I wonder how bad the leaks in the hull are.

Maybe the hatches were opened so the soldiers will have at least a chance to escape if …

HANDS

flip-flop-flip-flop-flip-flop-
   words-picture-words-picture-
   Everyone in the church has a fan.
   flip-flop-flip-flop-
   Everyone is fanning.
   words-picture-words-picture-
   It's hot in this small, midwestern town.

I'm not fanning. My mother next to me is fanning enough for both of us. Even though I'm getting a little breeze from the large lady next to me, I wish she was not sitting so close.

My fan is in the pew rack in front of me, and I pull it to me. I'm just learning to read, but I know my letters. One side of the fan has words, the other side has a picture. I ask my mother what the words say.

"Murphy's Mortuary" she reads to me. "We are here to help in your time of need"

"What's a mortuary?" I ask.

"Shhhhh," she says, "I'll tell you later."

I turn the fan over and study the picture. It's a man (I can tell because he has a beard) wearing a bright red robe, sitting awkwardly on a rock. It must be cold there for him to be wrapped in so many layers. But maybe not, because one foot is outside the robe and he has on sandals.

He is looking up at the dark and stormy sky. A shaft of sunlight is shining on his face, AND on his hands. The hands are not palms together as in prayer. Almost every home we visit in this little town has at least one picture of praying hands on the dining room wall. The fan man's hands are together, but clenched. Is he angry? I put my fan back in the pew rack, and experiment with different positions for my hands; palms up, then down. Palms together in prayer, then fists clenched. Hands up to my face, then down on my lap. I go on and on. At last it is time to stand up and sing a hymn. Everyone has to put their fans down.

As time rolls on and I grow up, the fascination with my hands also grows. I have to touch things. Words of warning are often thrown at me.

"Don't touch that!" Someone will shout. "It's nasty."

But how can I tell if I don't touch it? At least I'm no longer a baby who would put it in my mouth.

The memories of things touched now brings a smile to my face. When helping my mother cook, shoving my hand clear to the wrist into a ten-pound bag of soft, cool white flour. Holding my palms up to feel the tickling drops of rain. Stretching my hands out to feel the warmth from the fireplace.

In my early 30s, I started sculpting in stone. The surface of the marble had to be touched by my bare fingers to determine when the sanding and polishing were finished. The eye alone was not sensitive enough to tell. Stone talks to me through touch.

When I was in Italy to buy marble I would walk among the stone blocks scattered in a field selecting the right ones for my sculptures. I initially picked for size and shape, enough to fill a twenty-ton shipping container. But often, I would just lay my hand on a stone and it would talk to me. Sometimes, it would say,

"Me, Me, Me!"

Others would just give me a gentle hmmmm. The most exciting message a stone could give was a vivid image of a sculpture, locked within, that wanted to be created. All these moments of communication came through my hands.

When visiting Gaudi's Sagrada Familia Cathedral in Barcelona, Spain there was so much to see in the variety of colors, textures, and designs. What attracted me the most were the magnificent arches standing on huge blocks of granite. These blocks were from different quarries located all over the world. I had to touch the granite. With hundreds of people milling around, I had a quiet moment with each majestic granite base.

I was born left-handed. My parents, according to the best knowledge of their time, constantly corrected me by taking the spoon out of my left hand and placing it in my right (correct) hand. I learned. I also did not talk until I was almost five years old. Later, in a college Child Development course, I discovered that the forced correcting of a left-handed child often slowed speech development during his early years. Sometimes, I still have difficulty getting my speaking voice started.

I'm now primarily right-handed. I write, I eat, I work with my right hand. But my creativity is expressed by my left hand. It's the one I use to create the final details on a sculpture.

*   *   *

Now in my early 80s the image of the man on the fan returns. I have learned long ago that it was a depiction, foretold by the dark and stormy clouds, of Jesus contemplating his coming death, an appropriate coupling on the fan with Murphy's Mortuary. His face was serene, lit by a shaft of sunlight. I wish for that serenity.

The hands, in his contemplation of death, continue to intrigue me. Were they clenched in anger, or in frustration, or in fear? Perhaps the fists were made in determination or resignation? I have experienced all of these emotional responses.

I now have a neurological disease that has created havoc in my hands. My fingers are curled in on themselves, making a clenched fist. Only with difficulty can the fingers be straightened. Even then, they have very little strength or control to hold a sculpting tool, or a spoon. My fingers are numb, they have no feeling. At this stage of my life, the joy of touching is in the joy of memories. Some of my fondest memories are the caressing of my wife. Now, I can see her body and my hands on her skin, but the sensation is from memory.

Oh God, where is the serenity?

Slaves Spend Their Free Time Mending Their Chains
Welded steel & bronze figurative sculpture
14 inches tall

Heart of Lightness
Academy Black Granite with LED lights
10.5 feet tall

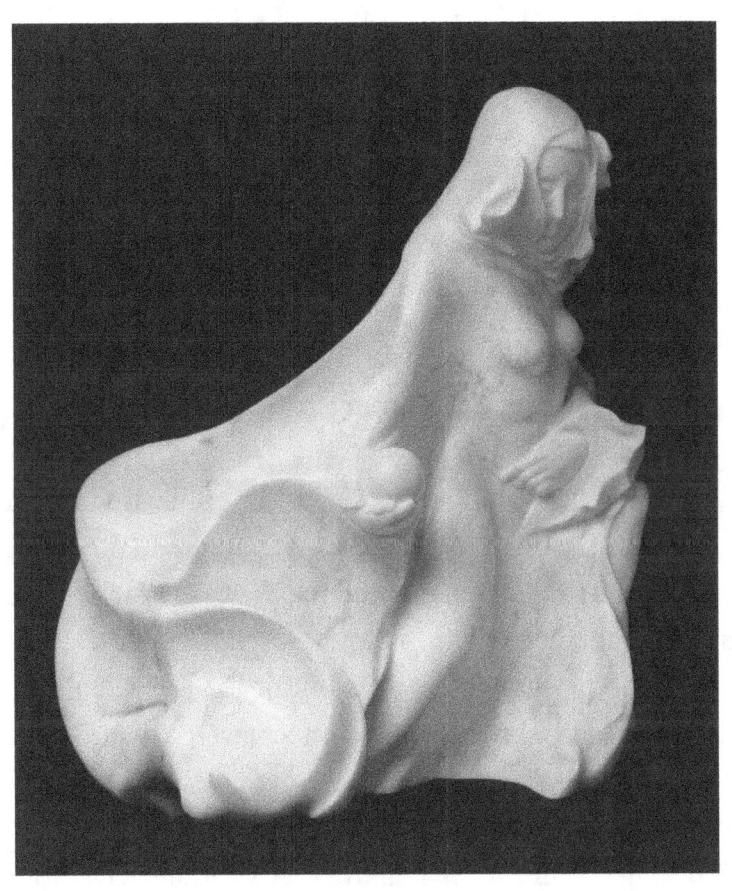

Demeter Searching the Earth
Statuario Marble
32 inches tall

MY FIRST SAIL

"You, sit there," Doctor Terry says to me, pointing to the forward seat in the cockpit of the small sailboat, "and do not move."

"You," he says to my dad, pointing to the other side. "Sit THERE, and DO NOT MOVE!"

This was the first time on a sailboat for either my dad or me. Doctor Terry, a friend of my dad's, had invited us to go sailing. On shore, he is a small, mild-mannered man with gray white hair and a slight limp.

As he gives the orders, he steps out of the yacht club's tender, drags a bag of sails with him, and climbs into the boat.

"One more thing," he adds. "If the boat goes over, stay with the boat, do not try to swim ashore. The boat will float."

This outing was not getting off to a very good start. Doctor Terry is acting like Captain Bligh. He moves about the boat putting on the sails. The boat is a very small sixteen-foot Snipe, open cockpit with deck seating. It's moored to a buoy in the yacht harbor. Once on board, my dad and I do not move. Doctor Terry sits down in the back of the boat, grabs a rope attached to the sail, and holding the tiller, looks at me.

"Release the mooring line and cast off," he says.

I know what a mooring line is, and I know what it is to cast off. Sea adventure stories were exciting to both my dad and me. The tales of Captain Bligh in The Mutiny on the Bounty and Men Against the Sea were favorites. We had almost finished reading all of the Horatio Hornblower books.

I reply with a snappy "Aye, aye Sir!"

I turn back from casting off, Doctor Terry smiles (for the first time) at me.

"You will make a good sailor," he says.

The day is hot, muggy hot, and there is no tropical breeze. Doctor Terry is reluctant to answer any sailing questions. He seems distracted. We return to the buoy, the tender picks us up and drops us off on the club dock. The men walk ahead, and I follow. So this was sailing. Not really, I had just gone for a ride on a sailboat. The only sailing I had done was to cast off. We walk past the boats stored on cradles and on to the veranda of the Yacht Club.

Doctor Terry had been a medical doctor in China in the 1930s. With the growing threat of war, he sent his teenaged son home to the States and he and his wife came to the Philippines. They arrived in Manila just in time to be caught in the Japanese invasion, only hours after the attack on Pearl Harbor. The Terrys spent the war in a concentration camp. Even though the Japanese needed Doctor Terry's medical skills, they resented him and tortured him repeatedly. My mother and dad, both college professors, and my sister and I came to war-torn Manila after the fighting in 1949. It was now 1950 and I was almost ten years old.

Returning from the sail, we three settle into the rattan chairs on the veranda. The waiter brings us three cold Cokes with straws. This treat is the highlight of my day. Dad tries to pay for the Cokes, but Doctor Terry says no, that it would go on his tab as a member of the yacht club.

Less than a week later, Doctor Terry asks my dad to go sailing again, and to be sure to bring his son. My dad tells me not to stare at Doctor Terry's legs and not to talk about the war. Doctor Terry wears the traditional outfit of American and European men; a loose white shirt, crisp white shorts ending with cuffs just above the knees, and white socks with sandals. It is hard not to look at his legs with their deep scars. One calf is almost completely gone. As the club tender approaches the sailboat, I notice the name on the back of the boat, *Annie Too*. This time, Doctor Terry is the first to step out of the tender and he takes the forward seat where I sat before. My Dad takes his previous seat, leaving only the back of the cockpit for me. Doctor Terry crosses his arms, and says,

"Okay men, you dress the boat."

Dad and I stumble around trying to figure out which sail goes where. My dad is very heavy and awkward on the boat, so I do most of the work. Doctor Terry just sits with his arms crossed, not saying a word, watching while Dad and I figure out how the sails are attached. We raise the smaller front sail. However, the small, pointy end is down and the wider part of the triangle is up; the first of many enjoyable learning experiences.

"Let's go sailing!" Doctor Terry finally says, the first words he has spoken during the dressing of the boat.

He doesn't move to the back of the cockpit, so I stay where I am. With a nod from him, I grasp the rope attached to the sail and place my hand on the tiller. Again he nods.

"Cast off the mooring line!" I shout.

Doctor Terry responds with a smart, "Aye, aye sir!"

We're moving, B A C K W A R D S!

I move the tiller from one side to the other. The boat swings sideways, the sail begins to pull the rope through my hand. Looking up, the wind has made the sail take a beautiful shape.

I pull the rope in a little, there is a small tug on the tiller, I hold steady. The boat comes alive! We are sailing!

I experience the most awesome feeling I have ever had! My whole body is wrapped up in this moment. I am a sailor, this, I know. Even though I can feel what is happening, it is not until years later that I have the words to describe this moment. Sailing is the profound experience of connecting the earth's two great fluids, air and water. Holding the sail's rope (the sheet) connects one's self to the sail as it reaches high into the fluid of air to catch the energy of the wind. The other hand on the tiller connects, through the rudder, to the other great fluid, the deep waters of the earth. You are the connection between the great fluids, and, you are in control. You are the master of your ship!

Doctor Terry becomes more friendly, making suggestions on how to control the lines and the sails. After a real sail he helps with the tricky maneuver of mooring to the buoy. This time as we walk to the club, I am interested in the boats on their cradles. I see the different shapes and can imagine how the water flows round the hulls. There are deep keels on some boats and center boards on others. And surprisingly, there is a great variety of rudder shapes. I know that I have a great deal to learn.

Again on the veranda, we are served ice cold Cokes, the waiter placing a small paper napkin under each bottle. After a moment of reflection, Doctor Terry tells us that he has a serious bone disease as a result of his wounds from the war. He must be back in the States under medical care within two weeks. In fact, he is traveling by Pan American Air Lines, a relatively new and expensive way to cross the Pacific Ocean. He picks up the small napkin to dry his eyes. The napkin is too small to blow his nose on.

"*Annie Too* is now your boat," he says. "Your Manilla Yacht Club membership is paid up for a year. I have only two conditions: one, you take care of my beloved boat, and two, you take over my job as administrator of all the mission hospitals built since the war."

So, my dad and I take on the ownership of our first boat, *Annie Too*. And my dad takes on a second full-time job. Even with two jobs, we have many wonderful days of learning and sailing. One lesson; when the sun goes down in the Tropics, often the wind goes down too. We have no motor, but we do have a paddle. Also, not knowing any better, we go out in three and four-foot waves, the solid water breaking over our bow. With my dad's weight on the high side, sometimes we get the old boat up on plane.

*   *   *

Since 1950, I have had over twenty-five boats, mostly sail. I can't remember the names of all of them, but I do remember the incredible joy of each coming alive with one hand on the sheet and the other on the tiller.

WHEN THREE WAS A PAIR

In the mid 1950s I went to high school in a small town in southern Illinois. This was corn country; dry, hard field corn, used for cattle feed. In the fall the corn was harvested by a mechanical picker. However, the machine was not perfect and left considerable corn in the field. This gave teenagers the opportunity to work gleaning after the mechanical picker was through harvesting. To do this work one needed a pair of heavy cotton gloves. The husks on the corn were dry and had a sharp, saw-toothed edge. Corn husking gloves came with an extra left hand glove, because the left hand always wore out before the right. The gloves were advertised as a "pair with a spare."

The town was located on a two lane, east/west highway which followed the southern edge of the last glacier. The farmland on the north side of the highway was level, rich, fertile, and productive. The farms had newly painted red barns and white fences along the highway.

The land south of the highway was rough, hilly, and the soil was composed mostly of gravel. The gravel had been dumped by the glacier as it melted, about 22,000 years ago. This was hard scrabble farmland.

The quality of these farms showed in the students that came to high school. The boys from the wealthy farms, and us town boys, wore light weight cotton slacks with a small buckle in the back, and brightly colored shirts with long collar points. The boys from the hardscrabble farms wore blue denim overalls. In warm weather they came to school barefoot, no shirt, and no underwear. In cold weather they wore heavy, black, barn boots, which stank from their morning chores—slopping hogs and cleaning out cattle stalls. Sometimes they wore a heavy coat, which also reeked from hard work.

There were about 120 students in my high school. Each year there were projects to raise money for the senior class trip, the whole school pitching in to help the senior class. Every year there was a discussion as to where to go for the senior trip. Usually, the class went to Springfield, the capital of Illinois, about 110 miles away. When I suggested going to Chicago it was met with a great deal of resistance. I wanted to see the museums, the art galleries, live theater, and maybe live music. But Chicago was a long, 200 miles away. It was like another world. There were students in the school who had never even been to the county seat, twelve miles away.

Gleaning corn was one way to make money for the senior class. On a given Saturday, after harvest, a group of about fifty high school students would gather to pick corn. There were very few students from the hardscrabble farms, they had their own work to do on the weekend. Possibly, they were harvesting their own corn by hand, their fields being too small, and too steep for a large, expensive, mechanical harvester to work.

I enjoyed the day of gleaning. It was great fun working together as a group, fortified by hot chocolate and sandwiches and dragging a gunnysack behind for the corn. Tucked in the hip pocket of our blue jeans was the extra left hand glove. The ears of field corn were much larger than the soft, sweet corn that people eat for dinner. The corn crop was left to mature and dry on the stalk, the husk was dry and curled back from the ear of corn. Usually, working from left to right, your right hand grasped the ear of corn, your left hand pulled back any remaining loose husk. With a twist and quick jerk of the right hand, the ear of corn came loose and was tossed into the gunny sack.

For those teenagers who had to work at home, harvesting by hand, the ear of corn would be tossed over their shoulder, without looking, into a wagon pulled by a mule, following down the row. On the far side of the wagon bed a "bang board" was mounted for the ear of corn to hit before it fell into the wagon, the sound confirming that the toss was good.

Even though the students from the hardscrabble farms did very little over the four years to raise money for senior trips, they still went along with their classmates. They were a part of the school; played on the basketball team and in the school band. For them, a trip to Springfield was an exposure to a bigger world.

Chicago was different, the city of fantasies, the Forbidden City, Shangri-La, and an almost impossible distance away. But my friend Larry made it. His grandparents came north from the deep South, and farmed the hill country of Illinois with a mule. Larry's father, graduated from high school, left the farm, and became a highly valued plumber in the community.

Often, after school, Larry and I would ride our bikes to his house. His grandmother still lived with them, and while Larry did a few after school chores I sat on the porch and visited with the old lady. She sat in her rocker and prepared her chew, not the big, thumb-sized plug of tobacco that men chewed, but finely ground snuff. The ritual of preparation started with the opening of a small tin of snuff, then spitting into the powder. Using the frayed end of a large wooden kitchen match, she stirred the mixture into a paste. She rolled a glob of the paste unto the matchstick, which she then placed behind her lower lip. Not in front of the lower teeth, they were long gone from the nicotine poison. The unburned match stuck out the right side of her face. She had a frequent need to spit into a coffee can, which she placed on the floor to the left. Because her aim was not too good and the spit often missed the can, I learned to sit on her right side to keep my shoes clean. The difficulty of speaking with no bottom teeth, plus her hearing impairment made conversation difficult.

Larry went to college and became a schoolteacher in a nice suburb of Chicago. The journey north took three generations.

While I was living in southern Illinois, my father had a 1955 VW Bug, there were no other foreign cars in the area. Chicago was the only place for servicing of this exotic car. So we drove the 200 miles to Chicago a few times a year.

Halfway through my senior year I moved to Seattle, Washington, over 2,000 miles away, to a high school of over 3,000 students. Once again I was living with the results of glacier movement. Puget Sound, Hood Canal, and the long north-south islands of the San Juans and the Gulf Islands in Canada had been gouged out by glaciers. The result was a boating paradise of harbors, bays, and coves.

I did not get to see the capital buildings in Springfield, Illinois. Nor did I wear out the first left hand glove of my corn husking pair.

MY PLAN

"What a beautiful day! I see why Seattle is called the Emerald City,"
I say out loud at the Saturday morning family breakfast table.

"Yes, and the mountain is out," says my dad.

"Boy, I'd love to go sailing today!" I say.

"Me too!" responds my dad. "Maybe today we should look at
the sailboat market."

"Okay," I say, "let's do it."

I have a plan.

I'm half way through my senior year in high school. Dad and I
had a sailboat which we gave up five years before when he took a
new job in southern Illinois. No sailing there for many miles. With
a potential job opening for my dad in Seattle, dreams of a sailboat
began playing in my mind every day. My parents and I planned for
me to go on ahead to Seattle to get into school as soon as Dad's job
was confirmed. I packed a go-bag. I was ready! The day after it was
official, I left the small town, hopped a Greyhound to Chicago, and
took the Great Northern Railway to Seattle.

The family I was to stay with until my parents moved out, met my train at 7:00 am. By 9:00 am I was cleaned up and walking a few blocks to my new high school.

"What can I do for you, young man?" asked the high school principal, backing her chair away from behind her desk.

She acted as if I was looming over her, as I stood in front of her. I was used to this kind of reaction. Over six feet tall and also wearing cowboy boots, I was big, my body hardened from a summer's work on my uncle's farm.

"I would like to enroll here as a senior. I just arrived at 7:00 this morning, and would like to start classes Monday," I answered.

"How old are you?" she asked.

"I'll be eighteen this month." I explained my situation. "I came out as soon as possible to complete my senior year." She knew the family I was staying with when I gave her their name.

Together, we walked around to the different classes I would be taking. I don't think she had ever encountered a student so eager to go to school. I knew it was going to be a real challenge to change high schools, and I wanted to get started as soon as possible.

Most teachers readily accepted me into their class rooms.

"What instrument do you play, and what position did you sit?" asked the band teacher.

"Trombone," I answered. "First chair in my high school, and also in the Dodge City Cowboy Band during the summer when I worked on my uncle's farm in Kansas." I didn't tell him that there was only one trombone in each of the bands. "But," I continued, "I would be happy taking 3rd or 4th chair."

He was very relieved at my accepting a lower position in his band.

However, the teacher of Asian History did not want me to join her class.

"We have already covered China," said the teacher. "And we are half way through the Philippines. Only Japan is left. I don't think you can catch up."

"I know I can," I replied. "Our whole family studied Chinese language, customs, and history at Yale University. My parents were going to China to be professors at Nan King University. We didn't go because of the political situation there, but went to the Philippines instead."

The teacher let me join her class.

My dad had given me the task of finding a sailboat when I relocated to Seattle. For the two or three months before my folks arrived, I spent much of my free time becoming knowledgeable of the boat yards and small boat sales in Seattle. When dad arrived, he became so busy with his new job that he didn't have time to even look at boats. I had also found a used MG for sale, but my parents could not understand why a high school senior needed a car of his own. After all, there was the family car for use.

My plan was in place when they arrived.

"Okay, Let's go!" I say after breakfast. "Better wear sailing shoes, Dad, we just might get the chance to go out."

At the car, I take the driver's side. "I'll drive, I know the way to the boats."

Leaving Queen Ann Hill on our way to Lake Union, we drive past the high school. It's a huge building. The enrollment is more than 3,000, a big difference from the high school of 200 in southern Illinois.

We park at Doc Friedman's Marina on Lake Union. Looking over the railing above the water, Dad sees a beautiful, eighteen-foot sailboat tied at the dock below.

"Look at that beautiful boat!" he exclaims. "The Emerald Green one with red mahogany trim."

"Let's go down and look at it," I say.

Leading the way down, I arrive at the boat, step aboard and remove the canvas cockpit cover.

"What are you doing?" demands my dad.

"Come aboard Dad," I say with a grin. "This is *Susu*, an eighteen-foot Mercury. And she's mine. Let's go for a sail!"

Emotions flash across Dad's face. First, surprise, then pride in his son. As he climbs aboard, I see a smile of joy on his face.

My plan had worked.

We had a great sail, the first of many joyful father/son experiences.

And Dad did not have to look for a boat.

Test Bed,
A platform for
experimenting with
different rigging, sail
designs, centerboards,
and rudders.

A beloved companion
for over 45 years.

Always there, even
when I was messing
around with other
boats.

Annie Too, Ranger 20 Converted to standing lug cat schooner,
with both tiller steering and wheel steering inside pilot house.
Now owned by Mike Smith, Napa, CA.

Welton R, Built from a set of Iain Oughtred plans.
Modified with off-set centerboard for easy cockpit movement.
Now owned by Roger Slagle, near Port Townsend, WA.

MULE

"I love him. I do, I do!" sobs Clara.

"No, you don't," answers her mother. "You have a crush on an older man, a man who is your teacher and who gives you attention. You're only thirteen years old!"

"But I do love him," Clara insists.

"John is a Yankee!" shouts her father. "We do not marry those people. For your punishment, you will work in the fields picking cotton along with the—"

"Aren't you being too harsh?" asks her mother.

"No," says her father. "She must learn what's right."

In the pre-civil war South, it was the custom for wealthy plantation owners to hire a live-in schoolteacher to instruct their children. John Dole, an educated man from Pennsylvania, had been hired by Clara's father to teach her as well as her older and younger brothers. Instruction continued through the evening meal, where the children observed and learned the arts of conversation.

The one topic which was never discussed was the whole race issue, including President Lincoln's position on State's Rights. This made for some awkward moments, but John was a master of conversation, and stayed abreast of current events, as best he could, during his time in Tennessee.

By the time the dark clouds of conflict between North and South grew, Clara had matured into an attractive fifteen-year-old young woman. With the threat of war, John caught the last train north out of Chattanooga to return home to Pennsylvania.

Educated, John joined the Union Army as an officer.

*　*　*

"Hey Grandpa John," said ten-year-old year Carl, John's first grandchild. "Tell me about the Civil War."

"No," said John. "It was just too awful…so many, many men were killed."

"Did you ever kill anyone, Grandpa?"

Grandpa John sat on the front porch, looking out across the prairie. His grandson sat with him, fidgeting. At last, John cleared his throat, and began.

"Another officer and myself were assigned to ride through the hills of Georgia to assess the strength of the Confederate Army before General Sherman's devastating march to the sea. Since I had lived in the south, I could speak southern."

John continued, telling Carl what he had said to his partner as they rode through the hills.

"I told him," John said, "I liked the south for many reasons; the trees, the soft hills, the warm climate, but mostly I like the people. For the most part they are gentle and kind. I know a young woman, for whom I have fond feelings. I had thought of settling in the south, until this war."

John's voice trails off as he relives the war.

"But really Grandpa, did you kill anyone?" asks Carl.

John returns to his story, describing his assignment with emotion in his voice.

"For our patrol, we were dressed in buckskin and wore straw hats. From a distance, we looked like a couple-a-good-ole boys. But our horses had a US brand on their flank, and a Union issued carbine rifle in a saddle scabbard. Hanging below our hips, on each side, we carried a pair of Colt 44s. Since we held the reins in our right hand, we practiced our fast draw from the left side."

"Oh, wow!" said Carl. "That's a lot of guns."

"We were deep in a pine forest, the wonderful scent surrounding us. I was smiling, this was one of the smells I loved about the South," John said. "Two boys stepped out of the woods in front of us and grabbed our horses' bridles on our right side. 'Aw recon us'n need these horses worsen' you do,' said the older of the fellows. 'Oh shit, you're Yankees!' He was armed with an old flint lock pistol," said John. "I couldn't tell if there was any powder in the flash pan, but I didn't take any chances. I gave my horse a little kick with my left spur. He jumped, throwing off the aim of the old pistol."

Grandpa John took a long, deep breath.

"We rode on." His voice broke with a sob.

After what seemed an eternity to Carl, who had never seen his grandpa cry, John continued, "I've never liked the smell of pine since then. I hope that you and your baby brothers never have to go to war. So many, many died. And now in Europe they're at each other again."

* * *

"Clara," calls her older brother. "Come quick. Someone's comin' up the road."

"Who is it?" asks nineteen-year-old Clara.

"Can't tell, sun's in my eyes. He's driving a wagon with two white mules. Could that be…?"

"John!" screams Clara.

Running down the road, her dirty bare feet raising little swells of dust, the frayed cotton day dress hiking above her knees.

"Oh John," says Clara through sobs, and tears, and smiles. "You came back."

As they walk to the house, John reaches out and holds one of Clara's hands.

"I'll put the mules up and come to the house," says John.

"You'll have to do it yourself," says Clara. "Most of the darkies have left, even though we told them they could stay."

"A lot has changed," says John, looking at the grown woman, and smiling.

A week later, Clara and John were married.

It had been a busy week; deciding what to take. California was a long way away, and homesteaders needed everything. John insisted on taking a cast-iron cook stove, even though it was heavy. "Good food," he said, "is important for our daily existence. And the stove will make food preparation easier."

It would make homemaking easier, and he knew how difficult their life could be.

"Clara," asks John. "You sure there's nothing else you want to take? There's still some room in the wagon."

"Yes," answers Clara, "I would like to take some of Tennessee, not today's, but yesterday's. You know, memories of earlier times."

At supper a few nights before, they had continued the discussion about migrating to California.

"News here in this part of Tennessee is hard to come by," says John. "But I've been reading the news on my way here. There's a great migration to the West building from both the South and the North."

"I would like to join you," says Clara's older brother, not looking at his parents. "I've always wanted to go to California. I thought my future was to carry on here on the cotton plantation. But now..."

"I want to go too!" says Clara's sixteen-year-old younger brother.

Her mother politely excuses herself, and slowly walks upstairs to her room. Her sobs of despair echo through the house.

With the morning sun at their backs, four young people, and two mules pulling a wagon, take the west bound road out of Tennessee, away from ruined plantations and sad faces.

*　*　*

"Hi, Grandma Clara," said her ten-year-old granddaughter and namesake, "I wish I had known Grandpa John before he died. I was just too young."

"He was a wonderful man," said grandma, now in her 80s. "And so happy to have a granddaughter."

"Why did you and grandpa stop there in central Kansas?"

"That's where the mule went lame," said the old woman.

Grandma Clara had come to live with her daughter and the growing family. A warm friendship developed between Clara and her grandma. Stories were told, family history passed down, and over time, Clara (my mother) passed them along to me.

With a lame mule, the plans of the four westbound immigrants had to change. They would build a soddy; a construction design unique to the great plains. Blocks of sod were cut out of the ground, and stacked like bricks, to form walls. Thus, the walls extended up from ground level about five feet. The inside room was below ground level where the sod bocks had been removed. Buffalo Grass covered the prairie, its roots so dense the block of sod held together to make a building material that would last for years.

The first winter in the soddy, a baby was born pre-mature. One of the prize possessions the parents had brought along was the heavy cast-iron cook stove. It became an incubator. In the evening, the fire raked out, the baby, wrapped in swaddling clothes, was placed in the stove to keep warm.

"I was so homesick for Tennessee; the trees, the gentle hills, and my own parents," said Grandma Clara, "I named my new daughter Sadie Tennessee Doles."

"Thanks Grandma," said Clara, "I've always wondered how Mom got her name."

The next spring, the young immigrants planted a garden. The vines of the pumpkin patch grew out over the soft grass producing more and more of the plump squash.

"The three men went away to buy cattle," said Grandma Clara. "Leaving me with baby Sadie."

Clara could see tears building in Grandma's eyes. It must have been a very difficult time out on the lonely prairie.

"There was a soft knock on the door. I picked up Sadie to answer the door," said Grandma. "There were two Indians, a very old man, and a boy. Behind them was a very thin, small pony. The old man rubbed circles on his stomach and pointed to his mouth."

Grandma paused for a moment.

"Hungry…I knew hunger…From the times at the end of the war."

She led the Indians to the pumpkin patch and indicated to them that they could have as many as they wanted. The man and boy braided rope from the prairie grass, tied the pumpkins on the pony, and walked away.

"Didn't they even say thank you?" asked young Clara.

"I'm not sure good manners were expressed in the same way as we do," answered Grandma. "But the next winter they did thank us."

Grandma went on to relate that the last Plains Indian uprising was held that winter on their homestead. For three days and nights the drumming continued non-stop, as the Indians held counsel to decide what to do about the invasion of their land by white settlers. The young immigrants (now five) hid in their soddy. When the drumming stopped, they peeked out. They had heard activity on their roof. A teepee was pitched on the roof of their soddy and sitting in the door flap of the tent were the old man and the boy who had been given the pumpkin crop. The placement of their teepee on the roof of the soddy had insured the safety of those inside.

Ten-year-old Clara was very busy, helping her mother care for two younger daughters. Since she was the first girl, she took on much of the cooking for the family. This included three older brothers, two younger sisters, her parents, any hired hands put on, and Grandma Clara, who moved into her daughter Sadie's home after Grandpa John died. The large Prairie Gothic home was barely large enough, even with three bedrooms on the first floor, five bedrooms on the second, and some sleeping cots in the basement for the hired hands. As the two Claras lived and worked together, many stories were passed down.

"At first," said Grandma, "I did not like Sadie's new beau."

"Why not?" questioned Clara, knowing her father was being referenced.

"Sadie, as a teacher, was living with a host family in town. David was just a hired hand for the farmer," said Grandma Clara. "He had no money, he had no land, he had no steady job, and he was supporting his mother and younger siblings."

"But isn't that a good thing for him to do?" said Clara.

"Yes, of course," said Grandma, "But you've got to understand. Sadie was a very good schoolteacher—maybe she got that from her father, John. And women were not allowed to be both a teacher and a wife. I can attest being a wife is a full-time job. Oh, oh, oh, the work I...we put into that homestead."

"Oh, my mind wanders. Where was I...?"

"Talking about Sadie's sweetheart, David," answered Clara. "How did his father die?"

Grandma continued telling about Clara's dad. "His father had had a farm in Gettysburg. The war had ruined the land for farming; too many trenches, too many dead bodies of horses and mules, but worst of all, were the bodies of dead soldiers. So, he took his family and joined the western migration. His Civil War wound never healed correctly, so he knew he could not do the heavy work of farming. He had been shot in the leg, but the wound did not heal. It just got worse. The doctors put maggots on his leg."

"Why did they do that?" asked Clara.

"The maggots eat the dead flesh, so new flesh will grow," said Grandma Clara.

"Oh yuck!" said Clara. "Sorry to interrupt, but I've got to start supper."

"Just let me finish about David's dad," said Grandma.

"He wanted to become a new Jonny Appleseed," she said. "He homesteaded in Nebraska. Land was cheap there, and he started growing fruit tree seedlings. He planned on supplying the trees to the western migration. However, there were two problems; one, trees do not grow well in Nebraska, you could see that by looking around. And two, the immigrant trails were farther south, mostly through Kansas. So, the father died and David, at sixteen, took over paying off his father's debt.

"Grandma," said Clara. "I really love the stories you tell, but I gotta make supper."

A few days later, both Claras were on the west porch.

"I love sitting out here," said Grandma. "Looking at the sunset."

"Me too," said Clara.

"I think it was the sunsets at the end of day that kept me from going crazy from the hard work, raising two babies, but mostly the loneliness. John and I would spend a few minutes sitting together each evening. He would hold my hand as we enjoyed the colors," said Grandma.

"I understand," said Clara, reaching out to hold her grandma's hand.

"You know," said Grandma, "Tennessee does not have the glorious sunsets. Maybe they were a gift from God to help me." She started to cry. "After a year or so, my older brother left. He always wanted to go to California. By that time he had his own horse, so he joined a wagon train as an out rider. I never heard from him again. My younger brother was so homesick that he up and left to go back to Tennessee. Never heard from him."

The two Claras sat quietly for a while.

"Enough of this sadness," said Grandma. I want to finish telling stories about your father, David."

Grandma continued talking to Clara. Her daughter, Sadie, was a very good teacher, loved David, and was also practical. She told him she could not marry him until he earned a high school diploma. So at twenty-six years old, David returned to school, studied, and graduated. They were married and purchased new land in western Kansas. They did not homestead.

"I'm so proud of David," said Grandma. "He has made a good life for my daughter."

*　*　*

"Grandpa David," I say. "Tell me what it was like moving onto new farmland."

I'm fifteen years old. This is the first summer I'm working full-time, farming my mother, Clara's, farm that her parents Sadie and David gave her. David is having difficulty driving, so I often drive for him.

"The first summer, Sadie and I camped out on the land in the back of the wagon, while I prepared the soil for planting. They called us 'sod busters' since we were plowing virgin soil," says Grandpa David. "But the sod, the prairie grass land, was so tough, such tight roots, that I could not plow through it with a moldboard plow."

Grandpa David continues describing that first summer.

"When planting time came, I wasn't ready. So I planted directly on the Buffalo Grass. Walking across the field, reaching into a seeding bag, taking a handful of grain, I would fling out my hand to broadcast the seeds in front of me." A grin spreads across Grandpa's face. "It worked! The wheat grew, headed out about three feet above the grass below. We harvested enough wheat that first year to pay off our land."

So began a lifetime of hard work, and abundance. Each year, he and Sadie bought more land. Eventually, they were able to give each of their three sons and three daughters a workable farm. That's why I'm here, in the 1950s, working my mother's farm, earning enough to put myself through college.

Many of the lifetime accomplishments are attributed to David, but I know that Sadie was involved in the decisions. When I was little, staying in the bedroom next to theirs, I could hear David and Sadie discussing their big plans. They believed in a healthy, educated community. The very best schoolteachers were hired, knowing that many would marry local men, and raise families with high educational values.

Grandpa David believed in community. Even though he already had the first steam tractor, when a workable gasoline tractor came into the farming world, he bought the first one in his community. He was concerned that the railroads were taking unnecessary advantage of the end consumer, charging the farmer exorbitant prices to deliver a single tractor. Grandpa became the Hart Parr tractor dealer in his area, bringing in whole train cars full of these seven-ton machines, and selling them at cost to his neighbors. His community grew and became prosperous.

When WWII came along, wheat farming became a vital industry. Grandpa and his three sons were very busy growing food. The sons did not have to go to war, and David was thankful for this. At the end of the war, The American Friendship Train was organized. It traveled from west to east, picking up corn, oats, and wheat donations for the starving people of war-torn Europe. Grandpa gave his whole wheat harvest (only holding back seed for the next year) to the Friendship Train, a total of five box cars, which added up to 75,000 bushels.

The IRS charged Grandpa income tax on his harvest. He fought it all the way to the Supreme Court and won. This is why, today, we do not pay tax on gifts.

"Grandpa," I asked one afternoon returning from Dodge City. "Why did you buy this car, a Hudson?"

"I liked it," he said.

"But why?"

"It had a flat head six, best engine on the market," he said. "I never did like a V8."

After thinking for a few minutes, he continued.

"I also liked the color, silver gray with maroon upholstery. But most of all, the streamlined shape spoke to me. It looked very modern. After driving boxy cars, the Hudson Hornet was my car. Not the most expensive, but the best."

Grandpa and I were looking for a special nut and bolt. I searched in the tack room in the back of the barn. The walls were covered with old, dried out leather harness, bridles, and other tack hanging on nails.

"Grandpa," I asked. "Why do you have all this old horse tack?"

"It's for mules," said Grandpa. "Not horses."

He began telling me about his experience with mules. At one time he had four pairs for a team of eight.

"What a job that was!" he said. "Each mule had its own personality. I worked with them when making up a team. They seemed to appreciate it, making harnessing easier when the mules knew who their partner was to be."

Grandpa continued talking about mules.

"You know, a mule is a hybrid between a horse and a donkey. Stronger than a horse, but they can be very stubborn. But I liked working with them, even though it was a lot of work taking care of them."

Grandpa David and I walked out to the pasture behind the barn, where old, worn-out, farm machinery had been hauled out and left to rust away into the original Buffalo Grass prairie sod. The machinery provided shelter to many small animals whose homes had been destroyed by plowing the prairie sod. It also provided a treasure of nuts, bolts, and other hardware. We found what we were looking for.

"I enjoyed working with mules," said Grandpa, looking out over the pasture, "but with a good gasoline tractor a farmer could accomplish more in a day.

We walked along in silence. I knew Grandpa was remembering his mules.

"When I bought a tractor, I didn't sell my mules. I turned them out to pasture here. They could make it on their own, but I did leave the barn door open in the winter so they could come in out of the cold."

I could see Grandpa's eyes were tearing. He really loved those mules.

"Whenever I drove the tractor pulling a plow in the field next to the pasture," said Grandpa. "The mules would run up to the fence and watch the tractor doing what they had done."

* * *

My mother lived for twenty years after my father died. Her final years were in a retirement home in Seattle. I visited her as often as I could, too much and not enough. For my last visit, we went for a "push" as she called it, in her wheelchair. Sometimes, we took a roundtrip ferry ride across Puget Sound. But that became too much. Today she resisted going anywhere.

"Come on mother," I said. "The trees are in their fall colors, just gorgeous."

And they were as we walked around the park.

"I love these trees," said Mother. "You know, we don't have many trees on the prairie and great plains."

"Yes, I know," I said.

We walked along, traveling on the sidewalk around the park. The front steps of a home across the street were decorated with pumpkins, gourds, and other fall items.

"They tell us," Mother said, "that the Indians taught the Pilgrims at the first Thanksgiving about pumpkins, corn, and turkey, all native to the new world. I'm not so sure, but it makes for a good story. True, but maybe not factual."

"Did I ever tell you about my Grandma Clara giving the Indians her whole crop of pumpkins?"

"Yes," I said, "but you can tell me again. Hang on Mother. The sidewalk is rough."

As we made it over the bump, we were showered with a flurry of leaves in their best fall colors, a gift from the same tree whose roots had lifted the sidewalk forming the bump in our path.

"Life is full of bumps," said Mother. "You just have to keep going; around, over, or under the bump, even if it's in a new direction. I sense a big bump coming up…"

Mother was quiet for a few minutes.

"I'm so proud of having been a part of the great western migration. It was truly a much needed joining of the South (my grandma Clara) and the North (grandpa John). They never made it to California, but you have."

"It was hard at first, for me to accept you being a sculptor," said Mother. "But that statement by Pearl Buck, you know, the newspaper clipping, helped me to understand you. Do you remember it? Do you still have the clipping?"

"Yes, I do," I said. "It has helped me to understand myself. Thanks."

We walked along for a while. I couldn't tell if Mother was asleep or off somewhere in her mind.

"Did I ever tell you," asked Mother, "what my Grandma Clara said when I asked her why she and Grandpa John stopped in central Kansas?"

"She told me, 'That's where the mule went lame.'"

statement by Pearl Buck:
"The truly creative mind in any field is no more than this: a human creature born abnormally, inhumanly sensitive. To him a touch is a blow, a sound is a noise, a misfortune is a tragedy, a joy is an ecstasy, a friend is a lover, a lover is a god, and failure is death. Add to this cruelly delicate organism the overpowering necessity to create, create, create—so that without the creating of music or poetry or books or buildings or something of meaning, his very breath is cut off from him. He must create, must pour out creation. By some strange, unknown, inward urgency he is not really alive unless he is creating."

KITCHENS I HAVE KNOWN

As told to me by my mother

"Breathe!" shouts Carl, her older brother, "Wake up. Take a breath."

I don't want to wake up, thinks eight-year-old Clara. I'm so tired. I just want to keep my head down on the table. Oh, my head aches so bad.

"Get up! Breathe!" commands Hugh, her favorite brother, as he lifts and drags her out of the kitchen to the screened-in porch. He sets her down on the long bench the men use to take off their work shoes before coming into the house, again he says, "Breathe, breathe, breathe."

"Why are you doing this?" Clara asks. "It's freezing out here."

It's the winter of 1920, very cold on the high plains of western Kansas. The large, prairie Gothic house is impossible to heat, so the whole family has stayed in the kitchen after supper. The room is crowded with the two parents, three teenaged boys, and three younger girls. The room is heated by the recently installed new, modern kitchen stove fueled by bottled gas. The oven and all the burners are turned on high. In addition, two or three kerosene lamps are turned up to their brightest.

Carl, the oldest brother at sixteen, pulls himself out of his stupor to go and relieve himself. Alarmed, he notices everyone is laying about, some on the floor, and the flame in the lamps is burning low. The oxygen in the room has almost been used up!

My mother Clara, loved to tell stories of her childhood on the Great Plains of western Kansas. But even more so, she enjoyed telling of kitchens she had known. These are some of those stories, told to me over the years.

The home she grew up in actually had two kitchens. The main one was used year-round. The second kitchen was at the far end of the screened-in porch. It boasted a very large cast iron range, with six burners and an oven that could hold a turkey. There were two or three tables in the room. This kitchen was used in the summer. The heat from the large stove was kept out of the house. Meals were prepared and served on the long tables.

It was a big job cooking for the family plus six or eight hired hands employed for the summer. This room also served as the laundry. Wash water was heated on a smaller "laundry stove." The younger children had the chore of bringing in firewood and coal for the stoves and removing the ashes. Clara, the first girl, helped with the cooking from an early age.

The first home my parents had as a young married couple was in a small sawmill town, high in the pine forests of Arizona. There were plenty of wood scraps available from the mill for fuel. However, the pine burned very fast and the kitchen stove had to be stoked very often with more fuel.

One day, dad brought home some creosote-soaked wood hoping this fuel would burn longer. The wood was from railroad ties which had been treated with the petroleum-based preservative. When the new fuel finally caught fire, it burned so long and so hot that the top of the cast iron stove turned bright red and began to sag down. When the stove cooled, the top was no longer flat. This surface was a real challenge for the cook.

The only time I ever saw my mother really cry was the day before we left our home of three years in upstate New York. The kitchen had a cast iron cook stove, and a very high ceiling with a system of ropes to hang laundry to dry. There was also an ice box, a wooden chest about three feet tall. Inside the top a zinc tray held a large block of ice. In the middle were racks to hold food, and at the bottom was a second zinc tray to catch the melted ice water. An iceman would deliver a block every two or three days. However, the bottom tray had to be emptied twice a day. A job which always resulted in a mess of water on the floor because the tray was often too full.

Mother was working as the dietitian in the school cafeteria, planning and preparing lunches for grades one through twelve. She was very concerned about cleanliness and food storage. The school had a large, electric refrigerator. It bothered her that the food for her own family was cooled in an ice box.

It was the end of WWII and manufactured items were just beginning to be available. The day before we left, a beautiful, new electric refrigerator was delivered to the house for the next family. Mother cried.

My dad was a Presbyterian minister with a Ph.D. in Rural Sociology, thus his interest in small, rural churches. It also meant we moved every few years. A large portion of his salary was paid by the national board of the church. In 1947, my mother and dad were asked to go to China to help rebuild the University of NanKing, which had been destroyed in the war. We moved to New Haven, Connecticut for my parents to study Chinese at Yale University.

Our family lived in a large, old four-story house along with six or seven other young "missionaries" who were also studying Chinese. The first floor had two living rooms, a large dining room, and a kitchen. At the rear of the kitchen, next to the large back porch, was a servant's stairway to the attic.

None of the young students knew how to cook, so mother conducted cooking classes. I was now about eight and joined the lessons on meal planning (emphasis on diet), cooking, food presentation, and cleanup. There was a great deal of camaraderie in the kitchen. Mother stressed the joy of cooking and having a positive view of food preparation.

Because butter was so expensive, margarine was used as a substitute. It came in a one-pound plastic bag, very white, but with a small pea-sized color bud. This small capsule, inside the bag, was broken by squeezing and then mixed throughout the bag of margarine with more squeezing, giving the contents a nice buttery yellow color.

Mother had stressed the importance of the visual, including color, in the presentation of food. A discussion came up around our communal dinner table…does the color of butter really matter? Some members insisted that the yellow margarine was not butter yellow. Others thought it did not matter. Mother suggested an experiment. Blue food coloring was added to the margarine, making the mix green. However, it was not an attractive green, but a dull almost military drab.

No one would eat the colored margarine. It really did look bad! The point Mother had made about the visual was proven.

After a year and a half of delays and more delays, it appeared that China was going to fall to the Communist take-over. My parents were redirected to the Philippine Islands. My dad was to be a college professor and director of the mission hospitals throughout the Islands. Mother took on the job of dietitian at the large inner-city hospital in Manila.

In our home we had three helpers: a cook, a laundry person, and a housekeeper who also helped in the kitchen. Mother would take the cook with her to the large, open-air markets to learn what was available. The vegetables were of course different from those grown in the US. At that time, right after the war, there was a law prohibiting the killing of an animal   who was still able to reproduce. So red meat was scarce and if available, was very tough. However, there was a great variety of fresh fish, which became a staple in our home meals.

Early, in the cool of the morning, I rode my bike to a local bakery to pick up a bag of Pan de Sal, bread of the sun. These small, sour-dough rolls were a welcome change from the usual diet of rice. After breakfast, and before going to work, mother would direct the cook to go shopping for the day. Our home was the "Guesthouse" for traveling mission personnel, so we frequently had guests for dinner and supper. I would often get home from school at 1:30 to find a dining table full of people.

At our table, a small bell was placed next to Mother's plate. Later, the bell was replaced with a small gong. Whenever something was needed from the kitchen, such as more hot rice or drinking water, mother would sound the gong to call a member of the kitchen staff. This ringing of the gong sometimes caused a judgmental discussion from the newly arrived "missionaries" who thought this was an insult to the "natives."

"We don't call them natives," my dad would say, "that's an insult from the 1800s, and European Imperialism."

The kitchen had a modern electric stove. The traditional Filipino cook stove was a shallow, clay pan to hold the fire under a clay pot supported above. Each item was cooked separately and set aside. The rice cooked last and thus was the only hot food. This stove evolved into a one-burner kerosene stove. This fuel was expensive. Mother insisted on having a four-burner electric stove. All the dishes of food, including the rice, were served hot to prevent the growth of bacteria. There was no hot water in the house, so after a meal the dishes were washed in water heated on the stove.

Mother was very concerned about cleanliness. We never ate raw vegetables, always cooked. One Thanksgiving, as a specialty, we had fresh celery. This was from a friend who had access to the US military PX store that sold items from the States. Another American family joined us for dinner, and we all were anticipating crudités of celery. Mother went into the kitchen and found that the cook had chopped the celery into small pieces and was about to dump them into a pot of boiling water! We had fresh celery, but in small pieces.

Ants were a big problem in the kitchen. Mother thought they were dirty. "Just think," she would say, "just think where they have been walking."

She may have been right. Over 80% of Manila's sewage was carried to the bay by open ditch drainage.

In the kitchen, the feet of the worktable and the feet of the screened-in storage cabinet were set in bowls of water to discourage the ants. Our pet dogs would always drink the water out of the small bowls even though they had their own water bowl nearby.

This problem was solved by adding a few drops of kerosene to the water of the leg's bowls.

*　*　*

After returning to the States, we lived in a couple of towns, finally arriving in Seattle, Washington. I don't remember mother talking about any of the kitchens along the way. Mother always tried to have something green included in a meal. Fresh vegetables were often unavailable except for cabbage and iceberg lettuce. We ate canned peas or canned spinach.

In my early days of high school, we lived in a small town in southern Illinois. One Saturday I ate lunch at a friend's home, his parents were from Appalachia. We ate one of the best meals I thought I had ever had; fresh side and gravy. I described the meal when I returned home. Fresh side meat, like thick sliced bacon but not smoked or cured, was fried until crisp. The pork fat was then made into white gravy, which was served over slices of soft, white Wonder Bread.

"Well," Mother asked, "were any greens served with your meal?"

I then received a short lesson on diet, and possibly why my friend and his parents were overweight.

*　*　*

After a few years in Seattle, Dad retired from the ministry, and took some short-term teaching jobs in Texas and Colorado. His last job was building the sociology department at Sheldon Jackson College in Sitka, Alaska. Mother again was involved in the field of food preparation, through a class of Sitka Indian women. She talked of how much she had learned about the cooking of game and fish from the women in the class.

The next kitchen mother talked about was in the Winnebago they bought upon their retirement. She loved the ease of that kitchen; cooking and shopping along the way as they cruised around the United States for a year. Their round-trip bought them back to the Seattle area.

One day driving to West Seattle to watch the sunset over Puget Sound, they discovered an apartment house under construction. They found that by purchasing an apartment now (the contractor needed the money) they not only got a reduced price, but mother could design her own kitchen! This was a first for her. For her whole married life, she had lived in housing provided by the church or college. It took another year to complete the apartment, but mother had a joyful time picking out the cabinets, appliances, and all the details of her own kitchen.

*   *   *

Dad died at seventy-six and mother became restless. They had lived a very enjoyable life in their apartment, but mother did not want to live there alone. She moved to Kansas to manage the food service staff in a large retirement community near Wichita. The conditions of retirement facilities in Kansas were appalling. She joined the state governor's Commission on Aging, and helped compile the state requirements for retirement homes, including modernizing their kitchens.

*   *   *

When dad was a minister in Seattle, he had chaired a commission to build senior retirement facilities. He directed the building of Park Shores, a retirement home on Lake Washington. To help raise money for the building, anyone could invest $5,000 in the project, and later they could move into the facility, their entrance fee having been paid in advance. My folks had planned on moving into Park Shores in about fifteen years, when dad was eighty. Now mother was approaching the time and decided to finally settle in the prepaid facilities. The entrance fee was now $15,000. Mother met with some resistance, but she was able to produce the original agreement.

She loved her new apartment. The kitchen was even smaller than the one in the Winnebago. It had a sink, two-burner electric stove, and refrigerator below...all in a cabinet two feet wide.

"At last," she grinned, "I don't have to cook anymore. The food service here is very good, and there is a friendly group to eat with."

Even though she rarely did, she knew she could make her own breakfast if it was too late for the community service.

Clara's life had progressed from helping her mother feed a family and farm crew of sixteen to twenty, cooking on a large cast-iron range, to a very small efficiency kitchen. At last, when unable to care for herself, she was moved to the infirmary floor where an attendant helped her to eat.

*   *   *

It had been almost two months since my last visit to see Clara at the rest home on the shores of Lake Washington in Seattle. At first, I didn't recognize the very old lady slumped over in a wheelchair. Was that my mother with the thin, white hair and skin so transparent her blood vessels showed through?

"Clara?" I asked, "Is that you?"

When I spoke, mother lifted her face and smiled that wonderful, warm smile expressing love.

The attendant brought lunch and she offered to share dinner (she still called it by that name) with me. I ate the cottage cheese with a bright red half cherry on top.

"Did I ever tell you about the high school kids and the Maraschino Cherries?" she asked.

"Yes," I answered, "but you can tell me again."

"It was in that little town..." Mother thought for a moment. "Oh, what was the name of it?" Again she paused. "It's just slipped my mind…there were so many little towns. Anyway, I was in charge of the food service for the whole school. High school students made up the work force in the kitchen; they were good workers. There was a gallon jar of Maraschino Cherries high on a shelf in the storage room. The level in the jar kept going down even though we were not using the cherries." Again, Mother paused. "I called together the crew and set out a bowl and spoon for each student. I invited the kids to help themselves to as many cherries as they wanted. BUT, they had to finish their whole helping." She laughed, "I even joined the cherry feast. I had always wanted to eat more than one."

"Well, none of us could finish…We were sick of the over sweet red cherries." She added, "The level in the jar never went down… and I've never eaten a Maraschino Cherry since."

We had a good laugh, and I finished my cottage cheese with the half cherry on top for decoration.

"You know," she said, "I could tell our food service here a thing or two. Maybe I should remind them," she said. "My Master's Dissertation was on institutional cooking. And, I have had some experience in that field. But, the food is pretty good…can't complain."

After lunch, I mean dinner, we went for a "push" as mother called her outing in her wheelchair. It was a cool, sunny fall day. The ground was covered with bright yellow, amber, and red leaves, making a pleasant swishing sound as we moved through.

"I wish," mother said after a few minutes of silence, "I wish I had written down the stories of kitchens I have known."

I had tried numerous times, during my visits, to record the stories, but she didn't like talking into a recorder.

"Mother," I said, "I will write the story of your kitchens."

She let out a little breath and seemed relieved.

"Good," she replied in a soft voice, "I'm 94, and ready to go. Sometimes I wish I were an Indian. Then I could just walk out into the forest and die."

"Well, Mother," I replied, "the forests are too far away, and you are too old to walk. So, you are going have to find another way."

*   *   *

A week or so later, I was in New York City and called mother to hear about her visit with my sister's family for Thanksgiving. After hearing about all the good food and family camaraderie, I told her a seasonal joke. It was about how the turkey, not the eagle, almost became our national bird.

She started to laugh.

Then she stated to cough.

Then to choke.

"Breathe Clara!" The attendant shouted. "Breathe, breathe…"

The phone went dead.

NOT GOING WELL

"Look at my ring," she said, holding out her left hand.

"Where's the diamond?" said her mother. "All engagement rings have diamonds."

I admit, it was modest. A simple Emerald (her birthstone) with two very small diamonds. The jeweler had insisted they were diamonds.

Actually, the very first thing she did before showing the ring was to introduce me to her mother.

"Oh, hello," said her mother.

It was not going well.

My girlfriend and I had driven from Portland, Oregon to a fishing camp high in the Rocky Mountains, to meet her parents, brother, and younger sister. We were tired and hungry. Her father had not yet returned from fishing on the river, so we had a supper of hotdogs and potato chips. We sat on the porch of the main cabin, eating our hotdogs, and swatting mosquitoes, talking about how beautiful the Rocky Mountains were compared to the hot, dusty flat lands of Oklahoma. We could not smell the wonderful mountain air because the kerosene lamps were smoking. Her mother said this would keep the mosquitoes away, but no one had told the mosquitoes.

The fishing camp had three very small cabins. The larger, center cabin had a small kitchen, with a sink, stove, and a table, one end pushed up against the open window. Behind a curtain were two beds. There were two, even smaller cabins on either side of the parent's cabin. The girl's cabin on one side, the boy's cabin on the other.

Her father returned from the river just as we were getting ready to go to our cabins.

"Hello, how are you?" he mumbled as he stepped onto the porch and pushed past us. I stood up and started to offer my hand, but he had a fishing rod in one hand and an empty fish creel in the other. He went on inside without stopping, clomped around, fished out a hotdog from the pot and sat at the table to eat.

I walked past the open window of the central cabin; she and her mother were sitting at the table.

"He's so young," I heard her mother say.

"He's 20 and I'm 24," my girlfriend said. "Not so bad. He's very nice and I want to start a family."

I stumbled and let out a little squeak. She had told me that she was twenty-two. Also, there had never been any talk between us about starting a family while I was still in school. When we met, she was on her way to Japan for a three-year teaching contract. I had three years of college left. It seemed easy.

However, less than a year after we met, she broke her teaching contract, and showed up at my door unannounced. She said she wanted to get married now.

She was the first woman I had sex with. I felt I needed to make an honest woman of her. An engagement ring solved all the problems. Yet…

Things were not going well.

Between her brother's snoring, swatting Rocky Mountain mosquitoes, and going over in my mind what I had heard her say through the open window, I did not sleep well. At first light I heard her father moving about in the cabin next door. Quickly dressing, I hurried out to follow him down to the river. When I caught up with him he turned.

"Where are you going?" he asked.

"I'm going to the river," I said. "To watch you fish."

"Fishing," he said, "It's not a spectator sport."

He turned and walked away, not saying another word.

Things were not going well.

Her father returned mid-morning. He had a smile on his face, and six very small trout. The limit for the day.

"I'll set the table," she said to her mother.

The table had a bench for two on each side, an old wooden chair at the head of the table, and the other end was pushed up against the open window. I counted five places.

"Oh damn," she said. "Where are we going to put you?"

The table was pulled out, a wooden apple crate was found for me to sit on, and I squeezed in under the open window. There was not much meat on a barely legal fish, but it tasted very good. This was the first time I had tasted fresh trout.

After lunch I tried to help clean up, but was obviously in the way. I stepped outside, her father had disappeared. This had been my opportunity to become acquainted, and to express appreciation for the fresh trout.

"Things are not going well," I said to her when she came outside. "It's time for us to leave."

"I agree," she said. "Let's go now."

She and I got married during Christmas break. I did not want to, but I was afraid I would lose her if we didn't. I had had very little experience with women and she seemed like the perfect one. So, I agreed.

For the first few months after our wedding, things seemed to go well... until they didn't. We had a fight over the use of contraception.

"You're just like my fiancé," she said. "He would not make love with me without using something. He didn't want a child. He left me."

This was the first time I learned that she had been engaged, and that she was not a virgin when we met. I was more upset that she had not been honest with me.

One day I discovered her diaphragm drying on the edge of the bathroom sink. She had cut a hole in it. When confronted with this, she cried and said she just had to have a baby. She had just received a birth announcement from her younger sister. The sister had a son at eighteen.

Things were not going well.

Our marriage didn't even last two years. I came home early one day from class. A moving van was just leaving, and in front of the truck I could see her driving away in our car. She was not a team player.

*   *   *

A few years later, while going through some old papers, I found a $25 savings bond with her name on it. We had each bought a bond with our wedding money.

I mailed it to her father. He replied, thanking me for the bond, and added that she had remarried, and still had no children. In a way, I still loved her, and was truly sorry.

Things were not going well for her.

TOOLS

In1960, I worked as a carpenter's apprentice on a huge bridge and clover-leaf project in Seattle. I arrived early with a few hand tools, including a retractable steel tape measure, all rolled up in a thin cotton nail apron from the local hardware store with their advertisement printed across the front. The other carpenters were all wearing bib overalls with padded knees, two large nail pouches in front, a small pouch between (for small nails which were never used on this job). The right leg had a loop to hold a hammer, and the left leg had a small pocket to hold a six-foot wooden folding rule.

The next day I came to work with a new pair of overalls. I used the small pouch in front to hold my eight-foot steel tape measure, a relatively new product on the market. The other carpenters thought I should get a six-foot wooden folding rule. I showed them how easy it was to measure more than six feet with my eight-foot tape measure. But they were not convinced, having used the wooden folding rule successfully for many years. And also the narrow blade of the eight-foot tape was very floppy.

* * *

A few months later Stanley Tool had a full-page ad on the back of Carpenter's Magazine. It showed a man's hands holding a tape measure in front of his jeans. In one hand was the tape measure with "STANLEY 12" on the case. The other hand had extended the tape about ten inches. Below were the words; "stays STIFF longer." How could any fellow not be interested in this product? My new tape measure was a big hit on the job, and it fit snugly in the small nail pouch. And it did stay stiff for twelve feet with the new slightly cupped ¾ inch wide steel blade.

*   *   *

A year or so ago a designer met with my wife and me to measure for wall-to-wall carpet in our living room. I came with my new 1 ¼ inch wide, thirty-five-foot tape measure. It was heavy and a bit awkward, but I could measure any room. The steel tape certainly stayed stiff all the way across the room. As I was setting up, moving furniture so I could get a straight line between the walls, the designer placed a small device about the size of a cell phone in the center of the room. It was a laser measuring device. Before I had taken my first measurement, he had the whole room measured with all the dimensions downloaded to his iPad. I put my large, heavy tape measure away in a drawer and have not used it since.

SCAB RAT

I am standing on the top of an eight-foot stepladder. On the top step, you know, the one that says, "DO NOT STAND – NOT A STEP." Noise, shouting, and swearing fill the side of the lobby. It's so bad that I am wearing ear plugs. My installation of the steel frame to support the water wall sculpture is going well. All the bolts are in, except for the last one.

However, the installation of the circular steel framework for the stairway, by members of the Structural Steel Union, is not going well. It does not fit. Some measurement is off. A huge steel I-beam scaffold has been erected, massive chain-falls to hoist the heavy frame are attached. But when lifted into place, the stair frame does not slip into the existing slot on the mezzanine level above the lobby. It is 18 inches too long, too close to the window. No amount of shouting, swearing, and beating with sledgehammers will make it fit.

The last bolt on my job slips into place. Out of my pocket, I take a small box end wrench, and proceed to tighten the last bolt. Below me, next to my ladder, a very angry man is shouting up at me. One more turn of the wrench and the bolt is tight. The man becomes even more animated. On my way down the ladder, I point to my ear and indicate that I can't hear. Even with the earplugs removed, the man makes no sense.

"You're a fucking scab!" he shouts.

Suddenly, the room is quiet, all faces looking at me. On the mezzanine the contractor is watching.

"He is the artist from California installing his sculpture," says the contractor.

"I don't care. No one is going to use a tool on steel on my job," says the angry man. "You brought a fucking scab to the job site. We'll bring a godamn scab rat to this job. We'll shut you down!" All the workmen are quiet, listening. They belong to the Structural Steel Union, a powerful union in New York City.

They could shut down the job. They could place a twelve-foot inflated rat in front of the bank's door at the Time Warner Building at Columbus Circle. They could stop all progress on the new bank office. No one crosses a union line blocked by a blow-up scab rat.

Pocketing my small wrench, picking up my few tools, and walking out the front door without looking back, is my solution to the anger. This is not my fight. I'm sure that the anger directed at me was the steel workers frustration over their job not working. Who could they blame? The architect may have misdrawn the plans, the steel fabricator miss read the plans, or the carpenters built the mezzanine incorrectly. I just want to install my water wall sculpture within the time frame given to me by the contractor. The large slabs of granite arrive tomorrow morning at 7:00 am. My steel frame is almost ready.

All the union workmen, except the cleaning crew, leave at 4:00 pm. Returning to the job at 5:00 pm, I am surprised to see a solitary workman still on the job. He greets me with a sincere apology for the way I was treated earlier.

"I'm an Ornamental Iron Worker," he says. "We are different from the Structural Steel Workers. Sometimes our jobs overlap, and that can cause problems, as with the circular stairway. Seeing what happened with the fit, I'm glad we didn't get that part of the job."

"Thanks, your explanation helps," I say. "Why are you still on the job after hours?"

"My job is very exacting, and it's hard to concentrate with all the noise and shouting."

"I can certainly understand that. What are you working on now?" I ask.

"I'm installing the curved metal trim in the back hall," He replies.

"Can you show me?" I ask. "I've always been interested in how a flat piece of trim can be bent into a curve."

Bill introduces himself. He is happy to show off his skills and the tools he uses. We have a few enjoyable moments of "shop talk" mostly about cutting, shaping and working with stainless steel.

"I have to get to work, to be ready for tomorrow," I say.

"I can't work with you," Bill says. "Our union rep doesn't mind me working after hours, but would not like to catch me working with another trade. However, I can help you carry your tools or materials. No one would know they were not for my job."

"Thanks." I laugh. "That would be a great help. Could you bring up the two, eight-foot-long, stainless-steel water delivery spouts from the storage area?"

Bill has never seen spouts like these, and he becomes interested in my job. He helps by holding up one end while I attach the other end.

After an hour of work, the spouts and their adjustment brackets are in place. With Bill's help, the water wall sculpture frame is ready for the installation of the granite slabs tomorrow. I pack up my tools.

Bill has stopped work and is eating his lunch. I too have brought a sandwich, and join him.

"I've always wanted to go to California," says Bill through a bite of food.

"Why?" I ask.

"It may just be a fantasy, but it seems to be an easier place to live."

"How so?" I ask again.

"The few Californians I've met seem to be more relaxed, more happy than New Yorkers," Bill says. "We all are so tense, so wound up underneath, just waiting for an excuse to get angry…like this morning."

"So why don't you leave?" I ask. "Take your skills and tools with you. There's work in California."

Bill looks down, and takes another bite or two.

"It's my wife," he says. "She likes it here. We live in the same neighborhood she grew up in. All her relatives are there. It's very loving and supportive, but anyone from outside is suspect. I can't imagine being an outsider in California."

"You may be right," I say. "Most Californians have come from somewhere else, and do not have that family support that you speak of."

I want to say that a person needs a certain adventurous pioneering spirit to move west, but that was not what he needed to hear. His wife certainly didn't have it.

We both are quiet for a while, finishing our sandwiches. The light is dim where we sit, off to the side of the work area. Bill speaks in a low voice, almost as if to himself.

"I want to say something. I've never said it to anyone. Not even to my wife." He pauses for a long minute. Takes a deep breath, then exhales.

"I had a job, a kitchen remodel," he recalls. "Only about an hour or so of trim work left. I had to wait 'til the other three guys finished setting the stainless-steel counter tops before I could add the final trim. So, not having to be at work first thing, I stayed in bed with my wife."

It is dark enough in the room that I can't make out the expressions on Bill's face, but his voice changes.

"On the way into the City, I was feeling great! I was in love with my wife, the job was over that day, I would have a few days off before the next job." Bill's voice breaks, "It was 9/11. My job was on the top floor of one of the towers. I could see the smoke from the bus window."

Bill is clutching and clutching again at his paper lunch bag. I know he is trying to hold himself together.

"I never saw my friends again," Bill whispers.

We sit quietly for a few minutes. The only sounds, our hands rustling through the brown paper lunch bags. Out in the street, a siren wailed through the night.

"I got off the bus and walked towards the towers. I watched as they came down. Emergency vehicles roared past me, their sirens screaming. I turned and made my way home," Bill said. "I've gotta get outta this damn city. Every time I hear a siren, every time I make love with my wife, I see those towers."

Bill stands up, throws his lunch bag into a waste can, and without looking at me, walks out the back door of the job site. Should I run after him? Maybe I could get him to talk more. Maybe I could encourage him to find some therapy. Californians are great for getting into therapy. Does NYC have help for 9/11 trauma victims?

I'm frozen, can't move. I've never been this close to the 9/11 reality. The short time together; working side by side, each on a ladder, sharing lunch time over sandwiches, Bill opening up about his longing to go to California, then his personal 9/11 experience, has brought me right to the edge of that day. The smoke, the sounds, the sight of the buildings falling, and knowing friends are trapped inside is now a part of me.

The scab rat, the shouting and profanity, all seem so diminished compared to the reality of 9/11. I look around, my job tonight is done, everything is ready for the slabs of granite to be installed tomorrow. Bill was a big help. I wish him well. I leave, making sure the back door is locked behind me.

The slabs arrive at 7:00 am and are installed by a stone fabrication company with union workmen. They do all the work. A few steel workers are watching, but they see nothing out of line. I never touch a tool. The threat of a twelve-foot scab rat placed in front of the Time-Warner Building has passed. This sculpture is the last of my six permanent installations in Manhattan.

TREASURE OF OLD PORT ROYAL

It's a story of a marriage that was not working...except this time it's my marriage. The divorce route was out. I had been there, done that. We were hoping a vacation apart would help.

I load my duffel, my tools and kiss my wife goodbye. She gives me a gift of a beautiful, expensive sheath knife with a seven-inch blade. The knife would be worn suspended from my belt at my back. It was to be a constant companion and vital tool for my time in Honduras.

*   *   *

A few weeks earlier, glancing through the San Francisco Chronicle, there was an ad that read something like:

WANTED investors and divers for work on existing

Old Spanish wreck off the coast of Honduras.

There was no phone number... only the time and place:

NO NAME BAR in Sausalito, midafternoon, in a few days.

Only a few guys show up. We sit around a table with a pitcher of beer and too many glasses, and introduce ourselves by first names. Tom opens the presentation with a few photos of a fifty-foot schooner. On her deck is a surprisingly small amount of dive gear.

He says that the schooner is anchored over the remains of an old wreck, supposedly Spanish. Jeff, his business partner, was in Spain doing research on this wreck site. Tom also has a few "old" objects that could have been found in any curio shop in the Caribbean. Three guys drain their beers, and leave.

The presentation concludes with the revelation that the dive site is on an island off the coast of Honduras. This was a known route of Spanish ships laden with gold plunder returning to Spain.

Suddenly, the mention of gold energizes the group. Those of us remaining sit up and start to ask questions. Tom brings out a magazine with an article about a successful treasure diving company in Florida that had hit it big. The photos of the gold treasure increase the energy level in the room. This is my first experience with "gold fever." Tom reveals that his dive company needs cash and experienced divers to continue. For only $3,000, still a lot of money in the 1960s, we could buy into EXPEDITION X. For this amount, we would receive an air ticket to Honduras and passage to the island. Additionally, there is an open return ticket for us to be used whenever we see the need. We would be fed as long as we stayed and worked on the dive operation. Any treasure found would be divided equally, those who had left would receive one half share.

I'm thinking, where else could $3,000 buy an endless vacation on a beautiful Caribbean island? There is work to do, but I like to work. I stay after the others leave and ask Tom if EXPEDITION X has an experienced carpenter in the crew. He asks me if I could build a dive raft to hold the air compressor, dredge pump, and the diving equipment.

"Of course," I answer.

I propose that I bring my carpentry tools and a chain saw, all together worth more than $1,000, to the dive site, for a reduction off the $3,000. The tools would remain behind when I left. Tom seems very eager for me to join the company. The dive raft is the big issue, I think I could have proposed almost anything.

We work out a number of details. I arrange to meet him at the travel agent's office in a few days with the money, and to receive my travel tickets.

My wife agrees that a separation might be the best for us. Her good teaching job eases some of the problems we face.

I build a small crate for my tools, pack my bag, kiss my wife, accept her gift of the knife, and am on my way.

*　*　*

Three of us from the Bay Area arrive at a small village on Roatan Island. We are exhausted but excited after a flight to Miami, on to Tegucigalpa, a small plane to the island, and finally a jeep/bus ride through the jungle. We are met by a very tall, very white man wearing a sun hat, long-sleeved white shirt, and khaki shorts.

"Call me Joe," is his way of greeting. He turns, and walks down to a rickety dock with an outboard motorboat tied alongside. I came to learn Joe was a man of few words. He says that there was only room for two. I volunteer to stay behind as I have the relatively heavy crate of tools plus my duffel.

Next to the dock is a small store. I buy a Coke, literally ice cold as there is slushy ice in the bottle. It gives me an immediate rush! Maybe it is the caffeine or the sugar, or maybe these Cokes are manufactured with the original recipe including cocaine. This is the first of many Cokes consumed over the months to come. I mention to the shop keeper that I am the new ship's carpenter, and give him my name. Edward (not Ed) is his name. He says that he too is a carpenter, and pulls back a curtain to reveal a small, but well stocked workshop. We are immediately friends. Finally

Joe returns, loads the small boat with my stuff, and casts off for the fifteen-minute ride across the small bay to the ship. No words are exchanged, but then it is difficult to hear over the sound of the motor.

*   *   *

We had been told that EXPEDITION X owned a 120-foot ship, retired from the refrigerated banana trade. What we had not been told was that the ship was aground on the mud, the bow resting on the shore. Joe circles round the stern. Above me are the faded letters; *Isabella*. Alongside is the fifty-foot schooner which we tie to. We join the other two new crew on the deck of the ship. They look like they do not know what to do. Pointing to an open door, Joe says, "Paul is in there," and he disappears through another doorway into the ship.

We enter the room, a little hard to see coming in from the bright sun, and there is a man sitting behind a table. He does not get up. In way of greeting, he says, "Three? Is that all there is?"

I pull out a chair, sit down, and introduce myself. The others follow. We had been informed about Paul, a professional diver from Hawaii, who is in charge of the diving program.

"Where's Tom?" is his next question.

"He'll be coming in a day or so," I say.

"Shit!" Paul explodes. "Now what am I to do?"

The three of us don't say a word. Paul stands up, and moves towards the door. I almost laugh at his appearance. He is a man in his late twenties, with a buzz haircut, dark glasses, open shirt showing his diver's physique behind a gold chain. What took me aback was his short legs; his upper body was normal, but he stood almost a head shorter than the rest of us.

Before Paul reaches the door, one of the fellows asks, "Where's the men's room? I gotta take a dump."

"On a ship it's called a head," Paul lashes out. "But they don't work on this ship. I've got one on the schooner, but you can't use it. It's mine. I live there, and it's private."

As Paul moves closer to the door and the light, I can see his face better. Below his dark glasses, his mouth looks like a pit bull ready to attack.

It seemed that Paul was going to be a big problem, with his lack of relationship skills. But as it turned out, Paul was only interested in diving, and I was a vital part of keeping the dive operation functioning. We ended up working well together, each respecting the other's talents.

After this meeting with Paul, I initiated my first ship's carpenter job—the building of an outhouse. The other two crew set about dismantling some of the old banana racks for their useable lumber. The outhouse stuck out over the side of the ship, complete with comfortable seating and thatched with coconut palm branches. There was even a door for privacy.

The outhouse was almost finished when Joe appeared and announced that dinner would be ready in half an hour. He also told us to find ourselves a bunk in the "officer's quarters" just behind the pilot house.

Two days later, Joe revealed that he had worked as a steward on a passenger freighter. Signing on to this expedition as cook, he also took on the job of making everyone as comfortable as possible. He was totally disinterested in diving for gold.

The next day, Tom arrives and immediately gets into a fight with Paul, who expected Tom to have a dive raft ready. Tom points out that he had sent down a carpenter and that the raft was going to be built ASAP. They both look at me, standing with the other new arrivals. We had just completed the outhouse, and were experiencing the joy of a job well done.

"My crew is ready to build the raft," I say. "We just need to know what's going on the raft and where the floats are."

Paul steps forward. "A dredge engine and pump, an air compressor for breathing, and various dive gear."

Two rolled up inflatable rubber "sausages" are brought up from somewhere in the ship. Unrolled on the deck, they looked pretty small. I do a quick calculation in my head.

"Won't work," I say. "Too small for the load."

Both Tom and Paul disagree, wanting it to work. So, for the next few days my crew and I build a raft. We run out of nails. I could have gone to town myself, but the crew needed a break. They were very ready for something different. I ask them to bring me back a cold COKE.

When the raft's finished, we slip the rubber floats underneath and fill them with an air compressor. It takes longer than expected, but at last the six of us launch the raft over the side. What a beauty! If we had had a bottle of champagne we might have christened the little vessel. All six of us climb aboard. It floats, but just. The floats are almost awash. Paul stomps off. Our combined weight is not even half the weight of the diving machinery. But at least we have a floating dock to tie the small boats against, making it much easier to get on and off the ship.

* * *

The days dissolve into weeks. Before Tom leaves again, I press him for specifics of when the new floats and dive machinery will arrive.

"They're coming," he says.

My two crew members leave, tired of working and not diving. More "investors" arrive, and more leave. I knew that Tom and his partner were trying to raise money, but we really needed to start diving.

Months later, I found out the delay was not the dive equipment, but trouble with the island's Commandant, the governor, who wanted ever increasing amounts of pay-off. He was holding up the delivery of the equipment.

My days are spent finding jobs on the ship that need doing. We completely rebuild one of the small outboard boats. The outboard motor was too small, so we install an inboard, air-cooled motor. I find an inflatable boat deep in storage on the schooner. The small outboard is installed on it. This gives us three boats to use.

Paul holds ongoing diving classes. We learn how to use different types of dive masks: snorkel, scuba (with tanks), and hookah (with an air line to an air compressor on the surface). This is the mask we will be using while treasure diving. Paul is a good diving instructor, constantly stressing safety. Over and over we practice taking off our mask underwater (or Paul comes up from behind and knocks it off), and then replacing it. Without panicking, we use our last breath to clear the water out of the mask and start breathing again. It takes some practice (especially the not panicking part), but we learn. At the wreck site we will be working in about 30 feet of water, not too dangerous, but a long way to the surface without air. It is crucial for us to learn how to replace our mask underwater. After class, Paul takes two or three guys out of the harbor to go spear fishing, a welcome addition to our diet of red beans and rice.

Paul finds sharing the schooner with Tom an annoyance, so he moves to town, rents a room, and installs a local "girlfriend." Tom objected, knowing this "in town arrangement" would cause dissension within the crew. But what could be done? Paul was the dive master. Hopefully, we would move to the dive site soon and the girl would be left behind in town.

Afternoon was the time to walk around the village. My friend-ship with Edward, the storekeeper/carpenter grew as we talked "shop." He invited me to his home to fix his wife's sewing machine. I was an utter failure at this, even though I could remember working on my mother's Singer.

We are asked over and over: just what are we doing here on Roatan Island? The official answer: we are setting up to do under-water photography of new dive equipment.

I don't think anyone believed this, but treasure hunting was illegal.

For the most part, the people on this part of the island hated the Honduran government, or "the Spaniards" as they called them. There were three distinct ethnic groups on the island. One, a group whose ancestors were a mix of Spanish and indigenous people (who had been enslaved by the Spanish). And another, from the time of old English pirates, many of who had intermar-ried with indigenous people. The third group was Black Africans. Many had descended from escaped slaves. The official language of Honduras was, and still is, Spanish, but on Roatan the people speak old English, almost Cockney.

There were also foreigners. One, an American farmer from the hard scrabble land of upper New York state. With the help of the government, he brought his farm equipment, his wife, and his teenage daughter to Roatan to grow vegetables, an item very lacking in everyone's diet. He was also a welder, a talent I often used in repairing our ship. After clearing the jungle, he planted chard and kale, both easy to grow. The whole town waited with anticipation for the first sprouts. One afternoon I met him in town. He was ecstatic. The crop was up! The next morning, I couldn't wait, so I went to see for myself. He was sitting in the middle of his field, arms hugging his knees, crying. During the night, the land crabs, also hungry for greens, had eaten every small plant. He was ruined. He had no money left, everything had been invested in this crop. The local boat builder also repaired steel ships, and needed help, so the farmer became a welder.

The back porch of the home of the local doctor faced the West. Many evenings, after taking a welcome shower, at his invitation, the doctor and I watched the sunset across the sea. He enjoyed talking with someone who read books, and I was fascinated by his stories of the island. One evening, after a number of visits, I brought up the Vietnam war. The doctor became very agitated.

"No war talk!" he cried. "No, NO!"

The story came out, slowly at first, then with a rush. It had never been told to anyone, but now he was old and wanted to unburden his past. He knew he had my trust. His story unfolded; he was Southern Italian, but now passed for Spanish. During WWII, when the Nazis invaded Italy, they forced him to join them and serve as a doctor. As the war progressed, he was afraid he would eventually be convicted as a Nazi sympathizer. With German papers, (he had studied at a university there) he escaped to the North into Germany. He joined a group of Germans who were escaping Hitler, leaving for South America. Not wanting to arrive in Argentina as a German, the doctor jumped ship somewhere in the Caribbean. He worked his way from island to island, finally settling in this little village, he married a local woman. Their daughter was studying in Miami. He took his wife's name as did his daughter. The doctor became very quiet.

"Thanks for listening," he whispered. "It's a big help. My wife only knows that I escaped Europe, as did so many. They will never find me."

*   *   *

There is an active fishing industry on the island. I come to know an owner after I give him a ride out to one of his boats. A few days later, he approaches me in town and asks if I would like to captain one of his smaller boats, a boat used for catching spiny lobsters. I say I know nothing about lobster fishing.

"You don't have to know," he replies. "Your job would be to keep those lazy bastards working."

I do not like his racist attitude. I say that I already have a job.

One morning, early, we hear someone shouting on shore near our ship. The man asks if there was anyone who could help him. By this time, our group had a reputation for helping the locals. He explains that he needs help butchering an old cow. I volunteer. My wife and I had raised a steer. Our place was in the country, and with the help of a USDA pamphlet on slaughtering and butchering, we had proceeded. This left a freezer full of beef for my wife and stepdaughters when I left.

So, with the experience of having done it once, I helped butcher. The rancher killed the animal with a sledgehammer blow to the skull. He was going to butcher the cow as it lay on the ground. I showed him how with a block and tackle and a notched board between the animal's hind legs, it could be raised up and we could work standing up.

I sharpened my beautiful knife with a few strokes on the stone, mainly for show as my knife was already super sharp. Together we butchered the animal. By the time we finished, there was a crowd standing and watching, many were carrying dish pans or pots, hoping to get a portion of meat. I said that I wanted the liver.

"Oh no," he said, "Not the whole liver, that is the most prized part."

He gave us about one quarter of the liver. I didn't really like liver, but that night the cook made the best supper I had eaten since coming to the island.

*   *   *

"Can I hold your knife?" Teenagers would approach me and ask. The reputation of my knife seemed to grow. The knife could cut through a 5/8 inch manila hemp rope, laid out on a wooden railing, with a single downward slash. The cut was clean, not like a rope which had been "sawn" through. I wore it everywhere, even when not working. I am over six feet tall, almost a head taller than the men of the island, and the knife, strapped vertically at my lower back, made for an imposing image.

The knife was long and slender, beautiful to the eye. The color was a soft, brushed nickel, set off with a deep black handle, quite the contrast to the rusty dark machetes used in the jungles. I confess, I would sometimes play into fantasies which were accumulating about the knife. I would caution who ever wanted to hold the knife to not even try to test its sharpness, they might loose their thumb. To emphasize this, occasionally, I would lick the hairs on the back of my arm and then shave them off with the super sharp knife. It was a lot of fun!

*   *   *

If we needed supplies from town, we hired a young man, the local contractor, who knew where anything could be found. He was always working: repairing a dock, pouring concrete for a generator pad, building a fence. He had a great smile. When working for us, we invited him to join us for lunch. He had a treasure of stories and gossip about locals. His favorite story, which I heard more than once, was his job of rebuilding a part of the waterfront.

A number of large ocean-going fishing boats were home based in this village. There was a lot of excitement upon their return

171

from weeks at sea. Friends and family would line the breakwater to welcome them home. Often, the boat's captain drove his boat full throttle at the shore, putting the boat in reverse at the last moment. This would cause a surge of water to rush up the shore and soak all the people waiting there. Everyone laughed and enjoyed the soaking. However, once (I don't know if it was a month or a year earlier) a fishing boat failed to shift into reverse and the boat ran up on the beach. It destroyed the dock, damaged the pier, and washed out a section of the breakwater. Our friend had weeks of work making the repairs.

We called him "Ki" because we could not pronounce his full name. He was proud of his indigenous heritage and took an Indian name. Ki had a sister, named Maria, who owned a small store at the far end of the village, near where the doctor lived. I often stopped there to purchase small gifts of Cokes or candy to give to the doctor for the use of his shower. Like her brother, his sister had a great smile. She was tall, and very attractive. We enjoyed a lighthearted flirtation which I thought we both knew was just for fun.

One day, Ki told me that his sister wanted me to stop by on my way to see the doctor. She was just closing the shop as I came along. Motioning to me to come inside she continued to lower the front shed roof which was also the outside door of the shop. As we walked through her living space behind a curtain, I noticed that her bed was neatly made with the top sheet turned down. On her back porch were two comfortable looking deck chairs. However, as I sat down my knife poked me in the back. There was no place for the knife to fit. I rarely used a chair; on board our ship, we sat on benches to eat, my knife hung down behind. Even at the doctor's porch, we sat on ladder-backed rocking chairs which provided room for the knife. On her porch, I wiggle around until I'm fairly comfortable.

Maria and I talk for a while. She had placed two lit candles on the railing, and in the glow of the setting sun, her beautiful face gives off its own light. She stops in the middle of a comment, and as she turns to face me, the white fabric of her blouse pulls tight over her breast. The top buttons are open and the soft light now makes the exposed curve of her breasts glow. On the tight fabric of her blouse is the faint shadow of her firm, dark nipples.

She looks at me, our eyes meeting. Then her question, "Are you married?" she asks with urgency.

As I reach over to take her hand, she grasps my hand in both of hers and presses my palm against her left breast. I can feel her heart beating just inside her chest. Leaning across, holding her breast puts our faces closer. I can feel her warm breath on my cheek. I also feel my sheath knife poking me in the back.

The question hangs in the air like a mighty sword guarding the entrance to a special and desirable place. I am hesitant to answer, and in my hesitancy, the light in her face fades.

"I am," I answer, "but it was not going well, so we have taken a trial separation."

"So you are available!" comes her quick reply. I pull back my hand and sit up straight.

"I would very much like to jump into bed with you. I know it would be great!" I continue. "But enjoyable sex is one thing. Getting the heart involved is another. I think I might fall in love with you, but then not be able to follow through with a commitment."

"Why not?" Maria questions.

"Because there is still a lot of love between my wife and myself," I answer.

"She doesn't love you!" Maria shouts. "She would have never let you go if she did."

Maria jumps up and pulls me off the porch, towards the door. She stops, throws her arms around my neck, and presses herself against my body. I'm very aroused, and she can tell. Letting go of my neck, she collapses on her bed, face in her hands.

"Get out, get out, you awful man," she sobs. I turn to leave. The bed squeaks as she jumps up, once again, arms around my neck, and a deep kiss on my mouth.

"I love you," are Maria's last words.

Leaving the shop, I stumble along towards the doctor's place. My mind is churning, wondering if I'm making the right decision about a relationship with Maria. I could find work here, and a place in the community, but would I be able to survive in this little village? The doctor sits alone, as usual, on his porch, seeming to be waiting for me.

"Thanks for coming, sit down," he says. "I've been thinking since our last visit, how much I appreciate being able to talk with you."

I sit in the rocking chair, my knife hanging comfortably down between the slats.

"I love my wife. But you may have noticed that she is never out here with us." The doctor pauses. "She gave me a home, a sanctuary from the war-torn life in Europe. She was a real beauty when I met her. Sex was great! But I have missed talking with someone about ideas, about questions." The doctor shakes his head. "She just doesn't have that."

As the doctor speaks, in my mind, I see myself fifty years from now, sitting on a back porch, enjoying a Caribbean sunset, saying, "I have missed talking with someone about ideas."

Walking quickly back to the harbor, I can feel the knife patting me on the back. I never see Maria again. I think she moved away, her little store stayed closed.

*   *   *

Maria and Ki had a younger brother, a teenager, who was a troublemaker. His name was José.

One day, as I come up on the ship's deck from working below a group of teenagers, including José, are standing by the railing. We kid around a bit and as they are leaving I notice a short cord, a lanyard, hanging out of José's back pocket. I grab the cord and pull.

"José," I ask, "what's this?"

"Oh, nothing," he answers.

But I know what it was, a distinctive braided cord attached to a metal point used for spear fishing. The barbed point catches in José's pants pocket. He turns to run to the edge of the ship, but I hold on. José struggles and his pocket tears. He turns and starts to blame me for ripping his pocket. I hold the cord out with the spear point dangling.

"José, you are no longer welcome on this ship," I say with a stern voice, "Get off, and do not come back."

I knew he was just a teenager trying to act tough, but this was one of the two precious points we had for the spear, the spear we needed to furnish food for our crew.

*   *   *

The next time I visit the doctor, he seems subdued. I wait, not wanting to intrude, until he finally begins to talk.

"That farmer friend," he said. "The one from the States. He asked me for some… (I didn't catch the name). I said I didn't have any, and why did he want it." The doctor paused. "He said, 'Oh, nothing' and left. I'm worried, in the past, that medicine was thought to cause miscarriage. It doesn't work, but makes a woman very, very sick." Again, the pause. "If his daughter, I think she's about 14 or 15, is pregnant, I can't do an abortion. It's illegal here in Honduras and, you know, word gets around, and I would be in great trouble."

After a long silence, the doctor tells me that he has connections in Miami and that if I could talk to the farmer, he would be able to help.

The next day, I meet the farmer (who was now 'the welder') at his lunch break. I repeat pretty much what the doctor had said. At first, there is denial. I interrupt, and ask him if he really wants his fourteen-year-old child to have a baby, and raise it in this village. He gets up, tells the foreman he is taking the afternoon off, and together we walk to the doctor's place. The story comes out. His daughter had been seduced (he didn't think it was rape) by the constable. She thought they were just flirting, just playing around when it happened. I leave him with the doctor.

A few days later, the farmer and his daughter go to Miami on the local freight boat, to get welding supplies.

* * *

A day or so after the welder and this daughter leave for Miami, I'm in town and see José and the constable arguing. When José sees me, he turns and leaves. In the past, I had tried to be friendly with the constable because he is the eyes and ears for the Commandant of the island. Some of the locals do not like us being in their village because until we came, there was no constable.

I ask him what is going on.

"That little sheet, he say he kill me." He laughs. "Ha, I gotta gun."

I ask, "Why did José say that?"

"I tol heem, I fook his gal friend." Again the laugh. "I say she a virgin…he not man enough to do it."

I say that that was pretty crude. He laughs. I turn and walk away.

Two days later, I take a trip to town to get a Coke. The shop is closed, but I can hear sounds coming from the workshop. As I walk around to the back door, I realize that the town is very quiet. Edward is bent over his work bench with his back to the door. When I greet him, he pauses his work and turns slowly towards me. He wipes his nose on his sleeve; he has been crying. On the work bench is a partially finished coffin. I place my hand on his shoulder, the tears start again. Then the story comes out, words spoken between sobs.

Early that morning, before light, the police boat roared into town, going much faster and noisier than necessary. It stopped at the public dock and something was tossed out. The boat took off. Someone was up early and went to see. It was the naked body, or what was left of it, of a person. More people came to see. The body was so badly beaten that no one could identify who it was. Eventually, as the sun came up, they could see that it was José, the teenager.

Both Edward and I are crying. Edward turns and continues working on the coffin, I pick up a tool and help to finish it. I return to the ship that afternoon, and tell the news, we decide not to go to the funeral. This was obviously an issue between the Commandant and the town's people.

*   *   *

A day or so later, I visit Tom in his office on the schooner. I can see pages of figures, some are spreadsheets.

"Tom," I say. "We gotta get outa here. We need to be on the dive site. The crew is not happy with the delay. Too many new guys have come, seen the situation, and left. Why can't we get the raft floats and the engines and move on to the dive site?" I add, that with the trouble in town, we do not want to be a part of it.

Tom explains the situation. All the equipment is in a bodega, a warehouse in Cox Hole, the main city of the island. And it has been there for weeks. Even though we were officially on the island to film new dive equipment under water, the Commandant suspected we were treasure hunters. When he saw the heavy equipment we had ordered, he knew. Now he was holding our equipment hostage for more payoff. Tom was hesitant to tell me what the amount was, the less I knew the better. But he did imply that in addition to cash, there were girlie magazines and guns. Tom admitted that EXPEDITION X was short on cash, but there were investors waiting for us to start the salvage diving. So it was a real balancing act. At this very moment Jeff was delivering a final proposition to the Commandant. If we didn't get the equipment now, we would shut the operation down and leave the island. There were other islands and other dive sites.

The equipment arrived three days later.

Meanwhile, the town held the funeral. I had talked with Edward about my not attending. He reassured me that the whole town knew I helped him build the coffin. Then in a quiet voice he shared a secret.

"The constable is gone. The door to the room he rented was standing open and his personal stuff, including his gun, was still in there." Edward throws back his shoulders. "Nobody knows nothing," he says with the faintest of smiles. "Nobody say nothing. Leave it be."

With that, I knew the subject was ended, never to be opened. However, on the ship, there was a great deal of speculation, mainly concerning the connection between José's death and the constable's disappearance.

* * *

Finally, it is moving day. There is very little tide change in the harbor, only six or eight inches, but every bit can make a difference in floating the old ship off the mud. Timing is important. The bilge is pumped dry. Three large fishing boats help pull us off. It takes the full power of the three, but we slowly slip out into the harbor. One captain had agreed to tow us down to the dive site. Taking our bow line, a three-inch manila hemp rope, the fishing boat starts to tow. The line parts—completely rotten. We are adrift, not a good place to be. The boat comes along side and the captain says he will tow us, but we will have to buy him a new line.

"Towing you," he says, "will stretch out my line and make it too stiff to use."

So we buy a 200 foot tow line, not cheap.

On the way down the coast of the island to the dive site, I take the wheel of the ship. I cannot keep us going in a straight line. I've been around boats most of my life, but those were small boats, not a ship. I knew the whole steering system was worn, the quadrant was slipping, making small steering adjustments impossible. But still, it takes skill and experience to handle a ship, both of which I lacked. I looked over, and at my side, Joe was standing there quietly. I ask him if he could steer a ship.

"Of course," he answered. "I have an Able Bodied Seaman's rating. I've spent many watch hours at the helm of many ships."

Thanks to Joe, we were able to pass through the narrow entrance with ease and were in the bay of Old Port Royal.

* * *

There were now sixteen of us on board, not counting Tom. The new dive raft, with its equipment, was anchored over the wreck site. Paul was in his glory.

He established groups of three plus himself to work one-hour shifts running the dredge. Everyone was eager to find gold! In each group, one person held the suction hose. The other two used their hands to stir up the sand with a cupping motion, the loose sand was sucked up by the hose to be discharged away from the site. Holding the hose was an important job; too far away and the loose sand remained. Too close, and the hose sucked up everything, including the gold treasure, if there was any. I took my turn and found it very boring.

Once the diving started, Tom announced that he was leaving to contact the big investors. He said we needed to elect a leader by vote. He would not vote, just tally the results. Paul spoke up to say he did not want the job since he was running the dive operation. Likewise, a retired air force officer declined…he had had enough leadership in the military.

There were no campaign speeches, no endorsements, just a call to vote. We voted, I got fifteen (I voted for myself) and Sandy got one. I continued my job much as before.

Tom left and Paul moved back into the schooner with his girl-friend from town. Paul and I streamlined his dive schedule. Each day, I made out a list of things to be done, and went over the list at breakfast. First on the list was how many divers Paul needed that day. It usually worked out to be twelve on rotating shifts. That left four of us to do all the support work. After asking Paul what he needed, I asked the whole crew if anyone had any needs, repairs, etc. Often it was nothing, but it made them feel like they were a part of the program. Sometimes someone would discover a repair that needed attention which I had not seen.

A typical day: Who wants to go for water? It was tiring, caring forty-pound jerry cans from a spring about thirty minutes up in the jungle. But someone had to do it. Water was a priority, so I never mentioned the next on my list until that one was filled. Next, were the small carpentry jobs. At last, the undesirable tasks. These were held back until all the rest were filled. I figured if no one wanted to do these jobs, I could do them myself. The worst was pumping out the bilge. It stank! Bilge water contains all the dead crap washed down over the years into the lowest part of the ship. The only light and fresh air is from an open hatch above. The small gasoline driven pump had a discharge hose up and over the ship's side. The intake hose disappeared down into the dark bilge water. Every few minutes, the hose would plug up and had to be cleared. This was a two-man job. One man pulling the clogged hose out of the stinking liquid and shaking it until the clog was free. The other man held the weight of the hose to ease the load on the first man.

Each morning, Sandy would not volunteer for any of the jobs that were on my list.

"Sandy," I said. "It's you and me pumping the bilge today."

Eventually, he asked me why he always had to pump the bilge.

"Because you never volunteer for anything, not even the diving."

He never learned, always waiting for something better.

*   *   *

The diving went on and on, day after day. Each day started with the hope that "today's the day!" For crew who were not on the day's dive team, there wasn't much to do. Other than pumping the bilge, I even had some volunteers. After the pumping was done, I took one or two fellows out to the reef to go snorkeling and bring back fish for dinner. We found that using a spear was better than a spear gun. A quarter mile offshore was a reef at about twenty feet deep, an easy dive with a snorkel. Beyond the reef was a steep drop off that disappeared into darkness. This edge proved to be the best fishing site.

The coral was more beautiful than any National Geographic photos. Fish of all sizes and vivid colors darted in and out of the different coral growths. Some I recognized from aquariums I had seen. The angelfish were among the most spectacular. They did not seem to be afraid of us, curiously coming close to investigate. Because they were larger than a dinner plate, our view through our masks was often blocked and we had to chase them away. Even at that size, they were only about one inch thick…no meat, and all bones.

Only the need to breath forced us to return to the surface. Within a few weeks, my lungs had developed to where I could dive thirty feet and do some work, before returning to the surface. I was enjoying my paid Caribbean vacation. No one seemed to mind my taking these outings to the coral reef, as long as I brought back fish for dinner and kept the dive equipment working.

*   *   *

A few weeks after we had moved our salvage outfit to the new site in Old Port Royal, we needed to resupply our gasoline reserve. We were in full operation; dredge, pump and outboard motors. A fifty-five-gallon steel drum of fuel weighs about 400 pounds, way too much for our small motor boats to carry. We had planned to take the fifty-foot schooner to town and load up on fuel, but that took a crew. No one, including Paul who was needed to sail the boat, wanted to leave the dive site. Today might be the day! It was also a lot of work loading fifty-five-gallon drums on the schooner. I said I would go in the small boat and bring back a drum of fuel, everyone laughed.

But I went anyway, with a shopping list from Joe and about 100 feet of half inch line. I took the larger of our small boats, a 25 hp outboard on a twelve foot boat with a load rating of about 300 pounds. In town, I tied up at the Texaco dock, ordered a drum of gasoline to be set out on the dock, and went into town to buy supplies. When I returned to the dock, a small crowd had formed, all wanting to see how I was going to carry the drum. The crowd was joking and laughing. With difficulty, I rolled the drum over to the edge of the dock. It was about twelve feet down to the water. My small boat was NOT below, but about fifteen feet away. I opened the plug on the top of the drum and sniffed to make sure it was gasoline. Then I replaced the plug and made sure all the other plugs were tight. I tied my rope around the drum. Now the laughing started in full roar! I could not help acting the dimwit; looking at the drum, looking down at the boat, playing with how hard it was to move 400 pounds.

Finally, I tied the loose end of the rope to the dock and just pushed the drum over the side. Big Splash! Howls of laughter! Everyone looked over the edge of the dock. I went down on my knees whistling and gesturing for the drum to come up. It did not come up! Now I was feeling a little worried. Finally, after about five very long minutes the drum slowly floated to the surface. Gasoline is lighter than the same volume of water. Taking the rope with me down to my boat, I tied off the drum astern, I joined in with the laughing and cheering on the dock, and motored very slowly back to base towing the drum.

How did I know this would work? When I lived in the Philippines (that is another story) my dad, who often traveled to remote islands, came back with the story of how some of these small villages were supplied with fuel. The drums were floated ashore from a freighter anchored offshore. The wind and waves carried the drums ashore.

* * *

Women, or more like it, the lack of them, were an ongoing problem with our group. Even though she rarely showed herself, we were all aware that Paul had a girlfriend stashed on the schooner below in his cabin. The reason there were always eager volunteers to trek into the jungle for water was that Paul's girl often went along. It was nice to have some feminine companionship. But even better was her bathing in the small pool below the spring. There was room for two or three in the pool, and she let the men bathe her. I don't think Paul ever found out, I didn't until much later.

Some of the crew would take off for a few days of R and R on the mainland. Once, two girls were brought back to the ship. It did not go well in the tight space of the ship. For those who are not participating, the nighttime sounds were a source of frustration. I had to say no more women on the ship. However, a few days later a forty-foot yacht tied up to our docking float, and without asking permission, a man and woman came aboard. They looked to be in their late twenties, and started asking questions about what we were doing. Our answer was, we are photographing new dive equipment…very hush, hush. The woman was beautiful and was acting extremely sexy, wearing the smallest bikini I had ever seen, even in pictures. It appeared to be made of only few strands of yarn. The crew gathered around while the woman was enjoying the rising testosterone energy. I took the man aside.

"I can't guarantee there will not be a gang rape here in a few minutes," I said. "You better get your woman off this ship, now!"

They got off. With the yacht leaving and the man steering, the woman stood behind him and took off her top exposing her beautiful breasts for all of us to enjoy. We all let out a primordial yell.

*　　*　　*

One afternoon while snorkel diving for fish, my diving companion speared a grouper, our favorite food, but it got away. The wounded fish went flip-flop, flip-flop down over the drop off into the darkness. We continued to hunt, about forty feet apart. Suddenly, but quietly a huge shark swam up out of the darkness, obviously looking for more easy meals.

Some of the crew had been divers in Hawaii and had experience with sharks. They related many facts about sharks, things to do and what not to do. Stay very still, do not thrash about or try to swim away. (I guess no one told the grouper that.) Unless they are excited or very hungry, sharks will circle around and around a potential meal. Then they will come in very cautiously to "taste" a meal. A shark tastes with the tip of its nose where there are many nerve endings.

So far, the shark is doing just what sharks do. I lay on my back, face and mask underwater, snorkel above the surface so I can breathe. I have big feet, size 12. My rubber flippers are also very big. I put them out in front of me. Hopefully, the shark's first taste will be of rubber. The shark stops circling and comes up to me. I can feel the soft touch-taste on my flippers. The shark is gigantic! Even with my large flippers side by side, I can see both eyes and all the way down its body. The shark backs off, then comes in again. It has not rolled its lips back to expose its teeth, so I know this is not an attack. I place the tip of my spear between my feet. You cannot kill a shark with a spear. When the shark comes in for a second taste, I give its nose three tiny pokes. We have a standoff. I don't move. At last, the shark swims away.

I swim slowly back to the boat. My companion is there, his arm resting on the side of our boat.

"Wow!" he exclaims. "That was a big one. I've swam with sharks in Hawaii and have never seen one that big."

I'm through diving for the day, very happy to sit in the boat and try to calm my heart. My companion heads back down to hunt for fish for dinner. As I relax in the boat, images of that huge head and the very small touch from the shark's nose replay over and over in my mind.

*   *   *

John, with all his boxes and crates, arrives in Port Royal shortly after we are settled into the diving. We work together building shelves and a work bench for his project. John was a retired Air Force officer, his specialty: electronics. We were the only married men in the crew, and quickly became friends despite our age difference. He had two sons about my age—one younger, one already out of college. Early married life had worked okay with his wife at home raising the boys and him gone most of the time. However, with retirement, John was at home. Finally, his wife threw him out.

"Get a job or something," she ordered. "Just don't hang around the house. You're bugging me."

He had answered the ad for investors and divers, and here he was on an adventure trip in Honduras.

As John and I talk, he relates telling the dive company he could build a magnetometer, an instrument to help find a potential treasure site. Tom and his partner are very eager for this to happen as soon as possible. Also, the big investors needed a good dive site.

John stops, realizing that he has revealed too much about the operation of the company. We look at each other. With a nod of the head, we smile. After a long pause, I look around to see if anyone else is within hearing range. We are alone.

I begin by telling him of my friendship with the old doctor in town, and a story he had told me about a horrifying salvage diving system used by the Spanish. They would take an indigenous man, tie a heavy stone and a 100-foot rope on him and throw him overboard. After three minutes, the man was hauled back up. If he brought something up from the wreck below, he was rewarded. If nothing was salvaged, the Spaniards would throw the man with his stone attached overboard without the haul out rope. Very effective.

The doctor knew what we were up to…treasure diving. Over the years he had seen many adventurers come and go. He knew the very site where we were going to start our dive. It was easy to find, and in fairly shallow water. The wreck had been explored many times. John and I discussed what we should do with this information. I said that I had suspected from early on that this was a practice dive site not expected to produce gold. Tom had encouraged us to keep a lookout for possible sites. Of course, there would be no timbers left on a wreck, all that had rotted away. What remained, and to look for, was a pile of round river stones which had been used as ship's ballast. Round stones in a pile are not natural on the sea floor. Supposedly, the gold treasure would be in the pile.

*   *   *

The days roll on. Moral is running low. As leader, I try to come up with a solution, but cannot. However, in the middle of an afternoon shift, just as I'm about to go fishing, we hear shouts from the dive raft. Some of the crew are jumping up and down. Two divers come back to the ship, the rest go down to work. They have "treasure!" with them! They had just found an iron spike about four inches long and a musket ball about 1/2-inch round. That night at dinner there is nonstop merriment. We are on top of the elusive treasure! If we had been archeological salvage divers, the two found items would have been analyzed, the chemical make-up of the metals studied and dated. But we aren't, we are proven treasure divers! To celebrate, Joe opens two cans of Spam. Sliced and fried it is a welcome treat.

The company's morale is back, but I'm feeling uneasy. I cannot express what seems to be happening to me.

My uneasiness continues. I go for a walk on a deserted beach, a perfect Caribbean day. My mind is relaxed in the surroundings. I notice, under water, close to shore, a pile of large, beautiful pink conch shells. I reach down about six or eight inches below the surface to pick up a beauty. Immediately, my wrist, and then my arm is wrapped with an octopus tentacle. My mind floods with images of an octopus at the other end of the tentacle, large enough to devour an old sailing ship. I scream and jerk back my arm, desperate to break free of the monstrous sucking tentacles. I'm frightened, no, not frightened, I'm terrified! As my arm swings back the octopus flies off, its tentacles spread wide, spinning like the hands of an out of control clock. It had seemed so big, and frightening, when it was attached to my arm. But as it flew through the air I saw how small it really was. It is all of about three-feet wide, spread out. I was frightened with the shark encounter, this was different. With the shark, I had kept my center and didn't panic. The octopus triggered a deep archetypical terror. All of my uneasiness found a focus in that terror.

*　*　*

John finishes the magnetometer and we try it out. It is crude, but works. We travel side by side, about a hundred feet apart, in two boats. Each boat has an identical instrument, checking on each other. A larger reading displayed in one instrument might indicate a find. For three or four days we troll back and forth across Port Royal bay without a serious reading. We are beginning to question if this system works, or if there are any wrecks down there. On the fifth day, suddenly, the needle on the dial of both instruments hits the peg. A few more passes over the area confirm that there is something, metal, very large below us. We mark the location to return with diving gear.

The next day, four of us return to the site with scuba gear. Fortunately, we brought an extra-long anchor line. The bottom is at 90 feet. At this depth, we are at the max for our scuba gear. But if it is a wreck site, it probably has not been salvaged. The water is clear and there is enough light to see. We are on the look out for the tell-tale pile of ballast stones. It does not take long to find the massive metal. Looming over us is a huge wrought iron anchor with one fluke embedded in the sandy bottom. It is hard to express excitement at 90 feet wearing a face mask, air tank, weight belt, and flippers. But we do! All of us are doing a dance of joy. John points his underwater camera for a photo shoot. I stand on the sandy bottom, the next diver on my shoulders, and the third likewise. Even with one fluke in the sand and the anchor at an angle, the head of the third man barley reaches the ring at the top. A huge chain drops from the top of the anchor to the sand below. We follow the chain, but it quickly disappears over the ledge and down into the darkness. Too deep for us to explore. Anchors are seldom lost, and if so, great effort is made to recover them. There must be the remains of a very large ship down in the deep, dark water.

*   *   *

That evening after finding the anchor, I told the crew the doctor's favorite story. He loved to recount how Morgan the pirate drove the Spanish out of Old Port Royal and Roatan Island. Details changed with every telling. I suspected that even the facts were altered, but isn't that often the way it is when stories are told?

The Spanish had built a small, but powerful fort up on the side of the hills above the harbor. It was high enough that no ship's guns could fire on it. Ship's canons were not designed to be elevated to shoot up. However, from its higher position, the fort had fire power over most of the harbor. Henry Morgan (the doctor was pretty sure it was he) wanted to continue raiding and harassing the Spanish outposts in the Caribbean. Old Port Royal was a vital staging area for the shipment of gold and silver back to Spain. By taking control of the fort, Morgan would command much of the Spanish gold delivery system.

Morgan had the cooperation of many of the other pirates and privateers in the Caribbean, so the doctor was not sure how many men were involved in the raid. Morgan landed his ship (or ships) on the isolated windward side of the island, the side hit by every storm. Cannons (the number changed with each telling) and the necessary supplies of cannon balls, gun powder, and all, were taken ashore. With a mighty effort, everything was carried, hauled, and dragged up and over the mountain. The cannons were installed above, aiming down on the Spanish fort. The dense jungle concealed the work.

Meanwhile, Morgan was sailing back and forth outside the entrance to Port Royal harbor. Inside the harbor, below the fort, a large Spanish warship was anchored, positioned to protect Old Port Royal's gold trade. The officers of the fort and of the ship prepared for battle. They must have laughed, knowing an attack by a single ship was a futile attempt. They readied their guns and casks of gunpowder.

The cannon fire from Morgan's crew took the fort below completely by surprise. The first blows were grape shots, clusters of smaller balls. The effect was much like a shot gun, disabling the wooden carriages holding the Spanish cannons. Of course, the casks of gun powder were hit and exploded. The warship was not able to raise their guns to fire uphill. The soldiers of the fort tried to counterattack uphill, but were thwarted. The English pirates aimed their cannon fire down onto the Spanish ship.

The ship's upper deck was not armored against shots coming from above. Some of the cannon balls broke through the deck and hatches, inflicting major damage below, exploding casks of gun powder, and setting fires. Chain shot—two half cannon balls linked together by a chain— destroyed the ship's rigging as the shot whirled through the air.

According to the doctor, the Spanish ship tried to escape out of range of the cannon fire. With its rigging damaged and on fire, the ship anchored in the mouth of the harbor. Morgan's ship came in, sank the ship, and continued with the destruction of the fort. To the old doctor's delight, Morgan continued to drive out the Spanish from Roatan Island.

After my story, the talk around the table became more intense. All we needed was a crew of hard-hat professional divers, and money.

*   *   *

The fishing dives continue. I invited Sandy to go out a number of times, but he did not want to snorkel, only scuba with his new tanks. With Paul's permission, I take company scuba gear for myself, and Sandy with his own outfit, out to the good fishing site on the coral reef near the drop off. Sandy had not taken any of Paul's diving lessons, because he said he had taken lessons when he bought his outfit. However, once we are anchored I go over a few basics. Always stay with your dive partner. Always swim up current so it is an easier swim back to the boat when tired.

We suit up, and Sandy goes over ahead of me. I hurriedly finish strapping on my weight belt, and follow. Sandy is swimming down current! I try to catch up. He turns to see me following, then continues down the face of the drop off. I had told him about the beautiful coral and their accompanying colorful fish, but he is not enjoying the scenery. I cannot catch up. Even though the water is very clear, the light is dimming. My scuba outfit is rated for 90 feet. I realize that I'm having to suck very hard to get air from my tank. I see that my face mask has a film of yellow over the glass...my nose is bleeding. Too deep! I stop, and hang suspended in the water.

What should I do? I cannot catch Sandy, I'm over 90 feet deep. I do not want to die. I float slowly to the surface, following my bubbles up. It is a long swim up current to the boat. After tipping my air tank into the boat, I cling on the side for a few minutes. Tears start. After getting in, I sit on the back seat sobbing. Should I wait? Should I run down current in hopes I could see his body floating up?

Making the decision as to what to do next is coming very hard. A hard bump on the side of the boat jars me from trying to make a decision. Sandy sticks his head over the side of the boat.

"What the hell you doing?" he yells. "You're supposed to stay with your partner!"

"Get in the boat and shut up," I respond.

*   *   *

That night at dinner, there was grumbling because we had no fish to eat, just red beans and rice. I apologize, but say there was a problem. I relate what had happened, including the yellow film on my face mask. I conclude by saying that I will never dive with Sandy again. For a moment the group is silent. Paul stands up, grabs and lifts Sandy who was sitting across from him, and with a string of profanity slaps Sandy's face three very hard times.

"You could have ruined this dive operation with your stupidity," says Paul. "Join this company, or get out."

Sandy leaves the table.

The next day, no one misses Sandy. At dinner, he is absent. Joe explains that just as he was casting off to leave for town early that morning, Sandy ran down and jumped aboard with only a small bag. He said he was going for some R and R, and would be back in a few days. I think we are all relieved. In the silence that follows, someone asks,

"Who's going to help pump the bilge?" It is a relief to laugh.

* * *

Early one morning, as I dress and buckle on my knife, I hear shouting and a woman's screams. On deck, a group is already gathering in a circle. Paul stands in the middle, one hand raised to slap. The other hand holds the girl's hair as she crouches on her knees. Paul is swearing at her.

"STOP!" I step into the circle. "Stop right now! What is going on?"

Paul lowers his hand, but continues to hold her hair.

"She stole it," Paul says through clenched teeth, "The little bitch stole the money!"

"No, no," the girl sobs. "I did no do it."

"Let go of her hair," I say, facing Paul, "And back off...NOW!"

Paul hesitates, then lets go of the hair, but gives the girl a shove. She falls flat on the deck. I see that her lip is bleeding. I say to the group,

"Does anyone know what is going on?"

"She stole the money!" Paul shouts, stepping forward.

"Back off Paul," I say. "And shut up!"

Joe steps up and says, "I was getting ready to go to town. I looked for the little money bag, it was missing. About $200. I came out and said the money was gone." Joe continues, "But just as I said it, the girl, with Paul right behind, came up from the schooner. Paul was shouting at her, but when he heard me, Paul then said that she had stolen it."

Joe looked around, but not at Paul, and added that he had planned to take her into town...And maybe that was why Paul was mad.

"Okay," I say, "Let's go to your office and get this straightened out." I reach out to help the girl, she jumps up, and the three of us disappear into Joe's small office just behind our meal table.

"Okay, Joe," I ask, "When was the last time you saw the money?"

"About two weeks ago," he replies. "I didn't need it for my trip to town last week when I took Sandy."

"Is there anything else you want to say," I ask. "Without Paul here?"

Joe looks around, and then at the girl.

"She comes up at night, after everyone is asleep, and helps me clean up. I know I'm not supposed to feed anyone but the crew. I just give her table scraps and leftovers. I would have to throw them out. And she does help with the clean up." Joe looks at the girl again, then adds,

"Last night, I could see she had been crying. She asked me to take her to town. She said she couldn't stay with Paul any longer. Of course I said yes."

"Thanks Joe, you can go. I want to talk with her for a bit. Don't leave without her," I add. "Just be ready in case Paul tries to stop her from leaving."

Joe leaves, and I look down at the girl sitting on the edge of the chair, her face in her hands.

"Stop crying," I say gently. "I will not let them hurt you. Did you take the money?"

She starts crying even harder.

"No, no! You look in my bag...no money." Through the tears she says, "I told Paul I love him, I want him to marry me. He laugh and call me a *puta*. Now I will leave him."

I say that is the best for her, because once a man hits a woman, he will do it again.

We leave the office, she follows behind. Fortunately, Paul is not in the group. I tell everyone that she didn't take the money. She goes straight to the waiting boat. Joe pushes off from the dock and starts the outboard with one pull on the starting rope. The sound of the motor brings Paul rushing up from the schooner. The girl is gone. Paul starts to scream. We all turn away.

When Joe returns from town that afternoon, he disappears into his kitchen. Over dinner, he says that Sandy is not in town. It has been a week since he left. No one seems to have missed him. One of the crew gets up and goes to Sandy's bunk. When he returns, he announces, "It's all gone. All that's left is dirty clothes, and…his complete scuba diving gear."

I'm thinking, trying to make sense of it all, when someone says, "Guess we just bought a scuba diving outfit for $200.

I think, not a bad deal, and we got rid of Sandy. But I keep my thoughts to myself.

*　*　*

It takes a while, but we get back to the business of treasure diving. The operation is running as well as can be expected. But I can feel a change in the air. Again, something is needed to re-energize the group. The excitement over the spike and musket ball find is wearing off. These "treasures" are mounted on the wall in our eating space. Those who are determined to find gold keep up the daily diving job. There are enough crew who want to go food fishing that I stay back and let them go. After the finding of the anchor, three or four of the crew join with John in his continuing search. He is happy for the additional help, and I'm happy to give them my place.

*　*　*

I had already explored the old fort site. Since it was visible from a boat in the harbor, surely it had been explored many times. There was not much to see, only rubble. There may have been more at the site, but it was overgrown by the jungle. However, I'm interested in the doctor's story of cannons being dragged over the mountain.

Going ashore with the fresh water crew, I set off following our stream up the mountain. The shipboard operation is running smoothly. There are plenty of divers eager to fish for dinner. Even the pumping of the bilge is covered by volunteers.

There is no path to follow, but the stream bed guides my way. At the top, the jungle opens out into a meadow. I cross over and find the beginnings of a stream flowing down the other side of the island. This meadow must have been a welcome discovery for Morgan's men, a place clear of jungle and large enough to gather all the supplies needed for the raid. Occasionally, on my way down, through breaks in the jungle I can see the beautiful, isolated beach spread out before me. It is like a glimpse ahead in time, giving little previews of what is to come.

The hike up and over has tired me. I mark the place I came out of the jungle so I will know where to reenter on my way back. I walk on the beach for a while, then realize that every step is the same as the one before. I have no destination. The beach goes on and on forever. It is like I'm treading water, afloat in this immense beauty. No travel brochure could possibly show the appeal of this tropical island. This is truly a primordial place.

Sitting on a coconut tree log with this beauty surrounding me, I try to take it all in. I feel that something is happening. I sense that my treasure hunting time is coming to closure. I don't know how it will happen, but "something is in the air." I believe in synchronicity, meaningful coincidence. I don't even know how to make it happen, but I do know that one needs to listen and be ready for the new to come along.

I begin to feel a numbness in my butt. I dissolve into the log. The colors; the different shades of blue in the sky and ocean, the dark greens of the jungle from which I had just emerged, the bright greens of the jungle in the sun light, and the dazzling white hot sands of the beach are all surrounding me and mixing inside of me like a painter's pallette. My dissolution continues and I become larger and larger until I am all that is around me. Time stands still. My presence there, or here, could be for a minute, an hour, or a lifetime. I am definitely a different person from my previous self.

Years later while studying meditation, trying to understand what happened to me on that secluded beach, I related this experience to my teacher. She said that I was very fortunate. Some people spend a whole life time trying to achieve what I had experienced. I had dissolved out of the physical realm and merged into the non-physical.

*　　*　　*

Joe greets me with two messages as soon as I return to the ship. One is from Tom, the other is a telegram from my stepdaughter. I look at Tom's first. Tom's note says that while talking with the freight boat's captain who had just arrived with supplies from Miami, it was revealed (to the captain's embarrassment) that he had lost an anchor in the harbor. Tom arranged for our dive crew to help find the valuable anchor. But we must hurry! The captain needs to leave. Bring the schooner and two divers ASAP.

Paul would be coming in from the dive site soon. I could work out the details with him then.

I retreat to the bow to be alone opening the telegram from stepdaughter. It says:

come back - stop mom needs you - stop
landlord selling house unless we buy it - stop

A cold chill wraps around me. Is this how fast the non-physical world works when not hindered by the barriers of space/time? I had begun to question my involvement with the treasure diving. I had listened. Here was an answer, not only about returning home, but also a way to get partway there. I didn't hesitate because I knew even before the telegram that it was almost time to go.

That night at dinner, I work out the details of the schooner, the divers, and say my goodbyes. I'm surprised that Paul is so eager to leave the dive site, but then I'm sure he wants a break and maybe to find a new girlfriend in town. I have my doubts about his chances, gossip travels fast.

Early the next morning I pack my bag, a small duffel. Not much to take home, most of what I had come down with has worn out. I open my belt to take off my knife. I notice my belt buckle is three notches into the belt. I have lost a lot of weight. I guess red beans and rice and fish is a slimming diet…at least, when the food is so boring one only eats enough to live on. It will be strange walking around through life without the knife patting me on the butt. I pull out the knife to cut off the old airline tags on my duffel. I look around in the dark, but can't find the sheath where I laid it down. It is time to go. I wrap the knife in an old shirt and stow it at the bottom along with a few interesting seashells.

Paul waits impatiently, the engine running. We cast off at first light. There is just one other diver and myself. Paul says that I might as well put in one more day's work before I leave the dive company. We power the whole way, so I never got to sail on the schooner.

We tie up alongside the freight boat, anchored near the lost anchor, and are met by Tom. He and Paul exchange strong words of which I can only hear the sounds, not the words. Paul leaves, getting a ride from someone heading to shore. The other crew member is a far better diver than I, and he is eager to use the scuba gear to dive on the lost anchor. My job is to stand at the bow, in sight of the diver in the water below and the freighter's captain up in his wheelhouse. It is a tricky maneuver to juggle the huge boat exactly right over the lost anchor, but at last the anchor is attached to the ship's cable and anchor chain.

The rescued anchor is slowly winched up, the diver swims back to the schooner, and I turn to leave. Tom steps up to face me, takes my hand in his, and grasps my arm with his other hand. I too reach out to hold his arm. We look at each other for a long moment.

"Thank you," he says. "We could not have gotten the dive operation started so quickly without your help and talent."

He pauses again.

"I truly wish," he says with emotion. "We had found treasure while you were here."

"Thanks, I had a great time." I smile and say, "And I did find my treasure." I told him I had discovered that I was a leader. I could take on a project, evaluate what was needed in the way of materials, and better yet, lead a group of men to do the work. I realized that I had the talent to lead and work together with people, even someone like Paul. (Tom grimaced.)

This treasure would support me for the rest of my life.

The ship's horn sounds a long blast, indicating that the ship is about to get under way. Tom gives my arm a squeeze, and without another word, turns and climbs down to the schooner. The ship's engines rumble, and we head out to sea, north to Florida.

In Miami, the finding of a drive-a-way car to California is easy. Seems no one wants to drive a car across country in winter, and the demand for drivers is high. With a car, I'm able to gather supplies for Joe and the crew, and deliver them to the ship for its return voyage.

On to Texas to visit my folks. My dad is a professor at a small college. When I meet him at his office, I can tell he is bothered by my scruffy outfit, my shaggy hair, and my long beard. In the hall on our way to lunch, we meet one of my dad's faculty members, and Dad is quick to explain that I had been treasure diving on an old Spanish wreck in the Caribbean. With a very snide remark, the man asks if I found any treasure.

"Yes, very much," I answer with enthusiasm. "But we can't talk about it yet."

I walk on down the hall. Over lunch, I tell my dad of finding my treasure, that I was a leader. My dad is proud. He asks what I'm going to do with my treasure.

I answer that I have given it a lot of thought. Perhaps, go back to school and finish my master's degree. But I really want to get my contractor's license, and build a construction company. But first, I'm hoping to put my marriage back together. I do not tell my dad of my experience with the nonphysical world. I did not have an understanding of it myself. The search for understanding and the incorporating of it in my daily existence has been a core part of my life for more than 50 years.

On to LA and the car delivery. The bus ride to San Francisco is long. Fortunately, it is a night schedule. My wife meets me at the bus station, her kids are in school. The meeting is awkward at first, each of us being guarded. It is good to see her, and I realize that I missed the sound of her voice. A year is a long time. I don't remember what we talked about, but when she drives into our yard it feels like home. Suddenly, I'm overcome with tiredness. It has been a long trip from Old Port Royal.

A shower is the first priority, my last bath had been in Texas.

My wife asks if she can unpack my duffel.

"Of course," I say, "there are some delicate sea shells somewhere in there. I brought them for you."

The shower not only washes away the grime of travel, but also relaxes the tension and apprehensions of returning home. Is she different? More important, I know that I have changed. Will we be able to fit together again in spite of our differences? I know that I will take a lead in working out our relationship.

After the shower, with only a towel around my waist, I step into the living room. On the table next to the day bed are my few meager belongings, the knife, and the seashells. On the floor is a pile of dirty clothes. My wife is smiling and in her hand, about waist level, is the sheath for my knife. She steps forward, pulls my towel loose, and still holding the sheath, puts her arms around my neck. The day bed is only a few steps away.

TOTO THIS *IS* KANSAS

"Wow! Look at that dark cloud!" I exclaim, leaning forward to see the sky through the windshield. "Looks like an anvil."

"Yep," replies Leonard, slowing the car, "We'll most likely get some rain." He looks out. "The winds here in Kansas blow in from the south, but our storms come from the north." He glances up at the sky. "That dark, anvil-shaped cloud is the cold upper air mixing with the warmer lower air. There's a lot of turbulence, a lot of energy up there."

It's Saturday afternoon, Leonard and I are on our way to play in the Dodge City Cowboy Band, in his '49 Merc, a welcome relief from a week of hard farm work. He plays the trumpet and I play the trombone. The Band gathers on a raised Victorian gazebo in the center of the city park. Our music program consists of "American music," you know, John Philip Sousa marches, Aaron Copland, and of course "America the Beautiful." After all, it's the likes of us Kansas farm boys who grow the "Amber Waves of Grain."

Gathered about the bandstand will be farm families from miles around, come to Dodge for a Saturday evening's entertainment.

They will spread their blankets on the cool grass under the shade of Cottonwood trees, a welcome change from the sun-drenched prairies and miles and miles of wheat. On the blanket is a large basket containing supper. Looking inside any basket, you would find: cold fried chicken, deviled eggs (if the chickens are laying), a large bowl of green (or maybe red) Jell-o with canned fruit floating, a two-quart Ball jar of too sweet ice tea, possibly a wedge of iceberg lettuce with a dressing made of mayo and catsup, and of course, apple pie.

Leonard and I ate before the drive to Dodge.

"I wonder if the concert will be canceled?" asks Leonard. As if to answer his question, it starts to rain. Leonard slows the car. It REALLY pours! Rain comes down so hard the wipers can't clear the windshield. We're still twenty minutes away.

The next happens faster than I can relate. A tree blows down across the road. We hit the tree. I'm thrown forward into the dashboard, no seat belts in those days. My elbow takes the full impact into the radio grill.

The head lights, still working, shine through the tree branches. On the other side, eighteen or twenty feet away, is a swirling wall of…of…stuff! There's a road sign going past, a sheet of corrugated barn roof, tree branches, and more stuff, some look like wooden siding. The sound is deafening! Like standing next to a moving freight train or near a jet airplane taking off.

Then it's over.

We just sit in the car. Leonard can't get his door open, a tree branch is wedged against it. I hurt. My band uniform, a cowboy shirt, is soaked with blood from my elbow. A highway patrolman comes by and sets out flares. He helps me put a large Band-Aid on my cut.

"Boy," he says, "You guys are really lucky. You should see what happened to the farm buildings just down the road from here. Lucky the tree stopped you."

The patrolman gives us a ride into Dodge. As we are leaving, each with his horn in hand, a tow truck comes to take Leonard's car into town. We are dropped off at a minister's home, the minister of the church Leonard's family attends. He agrees to take us home, an hour and a half drive for him. He drops Leonard off first. My uncle's farm is a quarter mile off the highway on a dirt road. The minister will not leave the highway to drive up that road.

"With this rain, that road is going to be pure mud. I'd either get stuck or slide off into the ditch. Sorry, you'll have to walk," he says.

I make it home totally soaked, very tired, holding my left arm across my chest to ease the pain, and carrying my trombone with my right hand. I leave my mud caked shoes at the door and go to bed. This was no Yellow Brick Road to the Emerald City. Just a slippery, muddy farm road in tornado prone western Kansas.

The next day, Sunday, I stay in bed. Monday I try to work, but I'm in too much pain to scoop wheat. I go to the doctor to have my elbow x-rayed, but no broken bones. Two days later and still in pain, x-rays show that my upper arm, just below the shoulder is broken. Harvest has started, but with my left arm in a cast I can't do my job as truck driver, the harvest job I have had for three summers. A truck driver has to scoop the wheat out of the corners of the truck bed when the truck load is dumped at the grain elevator in town, as well as scooping up any spilled wheat. An impossible task with one arm in a cast.

This story could be titled: "Tis an ill wind that blows no good"

Because of my cast, I'm given the job of driving a combine, a job that requires attention and focus but is physically easier. A combine is just that; a machine combining a cutter and a thresher. In the past, the wheat was cut by hand with a scythe, bundled together into shocks, then carried to a central steam-driven threshing machine to separate the grain. My Grandpa had harvested this way. Eventually, a cutter bar was invented, and that was combined with a threshing machine and the whole rig was pulled by a very long team of horses or mules. Finally, a gasoline engine was added and the combine became self-propelled.

The machine consists of a front platform containing the cutter bar and wooded blades on a reel to pull the stalks of wheat into the cutters. The cut wheat travels up the platform into the threshing drum which separates the grain from the chaff and the straw. This mix falls on to shaker pans, the kernels of grain fall to the bottom, then up into a holding bin on the side of the combine, and the straw and chaff exit the rear of the machine. A very complicated, but efficient process. However, each stage must be regulated and kept in sync with the other stages. The platform raised and lowered to cut the wheat crop at just the right height. The over the ground speed adjusted to meet the volume or density of wheat being cut, because the threshing drum runs at a constant speed and must not be overloaded. The shaker pan's speed has to be adjusted so the separated grain will not be carried out the back and lost with the straw.

During the first years of my summer work I had often taken over the driving of the combine while my uncle or cousin ran along behind, cap in hand, taking a sample of the chaff and straw to see if there was any grain being lost. They would resume driving and I would have to walk back to my truck. During my time of driving, for only a few minutes, I did not have to make any adjustments to the combine. So I had steered a combine, but not really driven one.

There are two combines on the farm. A very old one my uncle drove and a newer one purchased four or five years previously for my cousin when he returned to the farm after college. A new combine had been purchased this summer to replace the old machine, which was worn out and only cut a twelve-foot swath. The newer machine of David's cut a very wide sixteen-foot swath. The recently purchased machine cut a whopping eighteen feet! Even though it was only half again wider than my uncle's old machine, it was much more powerful and could travel over the ground much faster.

This speed required a much faster response from the driver to all the adjustments that were constantly being made. A combine driver's response was based not only on what was seen (height of the crop, the dips and gullies in the field), but being tuned into the screeches, thumps, bangs, and whees of the running machine. My uncle did not like the new combine; he could not hear the sounds through the air-conditioned cab. The adjustments on his old machine had been done by pushing or pulling hard on levers. On the new machine, many of the adjustments were made by pushing a button (which he had to learn anew). And the machine traveled too fast!

We add a knob to the steering wheel so I can steer with my left hand, my cast resting on the wheel. All the other adjustment I can make with my right hand and feet. I become a combine driver. My pay increases from $10 a day to the full pay of $14 and then $15 a day with room and board.

Toto, this *IS* Kansas! Not the yellow brick road to the Emerald City, but the yellow-gold fields of wheat ready to be harvested.

PETRICHOR

Crashboom…boom….rumble, rumble ….rumble

I'm in the kitchen with the lights on so I don't see the lightning flash, but I can hear the thunder. I love these storms!

"I'm going out on the porch," I tell my mother.

"OK," she says, "stay on the porch, because, …you know."

On my way, I turn off the overhead porch light, I can barely reach the switch. The porch swing faces the mountains in the distance, a perfect place to watch the storm. The glow from the kitchen light shines through the music room window opening on the porch.

I think that thunder is made by God rolling huge stones down the sides of the cloud mountains. Dad says that it's the sound of the air rushing back together, like a big clap, to fill the hole burned in the air by the lightning. Maybe, but I like my idea better. I have never seen a hole in the sky, but then, I have never seen any huge stones either. Or God either. But I have looked.

FLASH! I see the lightning strike in the distance on the mountains. I count.

One

Two

Three

Four

Five

BOOM….boom….rumble…rumble …….rumble

My dad has told me to slowly count after the flash, and that would let me know how far away the lightning had struck.

"Why?" I had asked.

"Because sound travels about one mile per second," he answered.

"But why would I want to know, and how far is a mile?" I asked.

"By keeping track, you can tell if the storm is getting closer," he said. "And the mountains are about five miles away."

Sure enough, five counts and the mountains are five miles away.

Another flash, and another count, only four. And another rumble. So the storm is getting closer. Dad rushes out to the car to close the windows. It's dark. I can hardly see the car.

FLASH! I can see everything in that flash of white light: the car and my dad, the whole front yard, and even my sandbox!

Again I count, only two. Dad runs back and joins me on the swing.

"It's getting closer," he says. "We'll be getting rain soon."

FLASHBOOOOM!

"That was really close!" I say loudly, my ears ringing.

"Very close!" he exclaims, "Look, the lights in the kitchen are out. Must have hit the power line." Dad calls out, "Clara! Do you need any help finding the candles?"

No answer, but through the window, we see candles are being lit in the kitchen.

It's raining, big heavy drops. We are on the Arizona desert, the rain is welcome. I breathe deeply. I love that smell! My whole body is stimulated. I can feel the rain smell. I am too young to have had very many profound experiences, but the smell of new rain encodes itself in my brain. It is a major marker in my life. I sit on the porch swing absorbing the life-giving scent.

My dad is a word man, he loves words. Everything needs a word, without a word, how can anything be communicated? Dad is at a loss for words, surrounded by the smell of the new rain. We sit taking in this joyful smell. I don't need to talk, I feel.

Later in life, I remember him pulling out one of the large red volumes of the Encyclopedia Britannica for an evening's read. By the time I was in high school, he had read through all 24 volumes … twice!

When I was younger, a few years before this storm, I discovered I could create the wonderful, mysterious smell. I would sit in my sandbox, on a hot day, and eat sand. I could taste and smell the new rain. My mother told me the washing machine drain pump wore out because there was so much sand in my diapers.

I don't need words…I have created!

The rain increases and the smell slips away. The water is running off the edge of the roof in many small chutes.

"Dad," I say, "I like the way the hills and valleys and hills and valleys of the metal roof make the water flow."

"That's called corrugation," says dad, no longer at a loss for words. "It makes the metal stronger so it can be used for a roof."

I forget the word for now. I'm watching and listening to the many chutes of water coming out of the hills and valleys of the roof. I love the way the water flow has been organized. The rain stops and dad says it's time for bed. He takes me by the hand, a candle in his other hand, up the stairs and tucks me in bed.

"So, you have learned a new word today; 'corrugation.'" He says, adding nothing about the new rain smell. How could he, there was no word for it.

A few days later, after supper, crawling under the large grand piano in the dark music room, I take one of my sister's metal toy dinner forks with me. I jam the tangs of the fork into the electric outlet.

FLASH! A beautiful blue/white flash.

Pain jolts through my body.

Boom! I hit my head on the underside of the piano.

The lights go out in the kitchen.

I have created lightning! And even a power failure!

*　*　*

Seventy-five years later, I'm sitting on the porch of my cabin in drought-stricken California. The weather app on my phone says that there are possible rain showers this afternoon. I wish. There is no wind, but there is a gentle rustling in the leaves. Looking in front of me at the flagstone path, dark spots are beginning to appear. I smell that wonderful scent of fresh rain. The smell triggers a multitude of memories, including my early years on the Arizona desert.

My computer is on the table beside me. I Google "new rain smell." I read that two Australian scientists, in 1965, coined the word: petrichor. The word is constructed from Ancient Greek (pétra) 'rock', or (pétros) 'stone', and ichor, the ethereal fluid that is the blood of the gods in Greek mythology. Thank you Wikipedia.

No wonder that even as a child I could feel the new rain, it is the blood of the gods. What would my dad have done on that porch swing these many years ago, if he had had a word that could be used?

The rain has become a welcome downpour. No lightning or thunder which are rare in this part of California. I sit back and think about the story I will write. My thoughts are accompanied by the many chutes of rainwater flowing off the hills and valleys, hills and valleys, hills and valleys of the metal roof above me. I enjoy the way the design of the metal collects the rainwater and shapes it into chutes, each about two inches apart. I know, I know, it's "corrugated roof." Thank you Dad.

IT'S NOT SO BAD

"It's not so bad." I say from the back seat.

My mother turns around to face me. "How can you say that?" she asks through her tears. She and my dad have been talking about the imminent death of the son of a friend. He was injured in an accident, has brain damage, and is nearing death.

"How do you know?" asks my dad, keeping his eyes on the road.

"I've been there," I answer.

Dad hits the brakes, pulls off to the side of the road and stops. There is very little traffic, and plenty of room beside the two-lane road.

"What do you mean?" he asks, turning in his seat. "Tell me!"

He has been the Presbyterian minister in a number of small, rural towns in the Midwest. Dad was a pastor; he visited the sick, offered counseling to those in need, and was at the bedside of those dying. "At the end of their life," Dad explains. "Often, just before they die, they relax and with a smile say, 'It is so beautiful.'"

"It really is," I say.

A year before, when I was 12, I had been very sick. My parents thought I might have polio. Our doctor thought it might be an allergic reaction to the rabies shots we all were taking. These shots were administered in the spinal column between the vertebrae, one a day for twenty-five days! On day thirteen, I woke up paralyzed. By the time the doctor made his evaluation and located the anti-vaccine, it was evening. I was in a coma. The pain was so intense I had passed out.

In the car, beside the road, I tell my parents of my experience.

"I awaken to discover myself floating about six feet above my bed."

As I relate my experience, I am reliving what had happened. "The bedroom door is closed, but there is a glow in the room." I pause, looking out the window, trying to put into words what is so very vivid in my mind.

"The glow condenses into a single point of light, a few feet away from me, in a doorway above me. I move through the door into a hallway. But it is more like a tunnel, with a gentle slope up." Again, I pause. My parents looking back over their seats, are listening intently. "I feel the presence of someone next to me, just behind my right side. He, or she, gives me a feeling of comfort. I am not afraid. All along the walls and even on the ceiling there are beings singing. Maybe they are angels."

"Then what happened?" asks my dad, restlessly moving in the front seat. He seems impatient for me to get on with my story; he continues to fidget. But I can't tell it faster. I'm reliving this experience and it is very powerful. I search for words to describe what happened to me.

"There is a light ahead of me, I don't know if it is the light at the end of the tunnel or someone with a lantern, or a beacon, but I keep going. I arrive at the end of the tunnel. The light coming through the opening is blinding bright." I continue, "I step out. I'm on the side of a mountain, looking down through a valley below." I begin to choke up as I relive my experience. "It is really so very beautiful," I exclaim. "The river flowing through the valley is a light yellow green, my favorite color. The trees lining the banks are different shades of green, some with bright flowers. I do not recognize the many colorful birds flying." I'm trying to keep from crying, remembering the experience. "The air is fresh with the smell of a dark winter night in upstate New York, two feet of snow on the ground and the flakes continuing to fall. All mixed with the hot, pungent smell of harvesting wheat in Kansas."

I can see tears forming on my dad's face. He too has shared some of these smells.

"The entity who is standing behind me, speaks softly, 'Do you want to stay, or go back? Either way is okay.' I pause for a moment, taking in the beauty, the valley, the trees, the river. And in the air the smells and the sounds of birds.

'I'm ready to go back,' I answer the entity.

"I open my eyes in my bed, in my room, it's still dark. The door to my room is closed. In the living room on the other side of the door I hear muffled voices. 'Mom, Dad, can you come here?' I call out. The door opens, you're silhouetted in the light. The doctor stands behind you, trying to see me. He was waiting with you to see if the anti-serum worked"

I didn't know what more to say to my parents there on the side of the road. All through my life, for the next 70 years, I have never been afraid to die.

The entity who walked with me on my journey through the tunnel still walks with me today, giving me comfort when pain is in my body.

Thirty some years later, after my experience, I'm at the bedside of my dad. The doctors have informed my mother and me that dad's body is shutting down and the end is near. He has an oxygen mask on his face and two or three needles in his arm. His hands are tied to the bed rail to keep him from pulling out the IVs. He is obviously very stressed.

"Can you hear me?" I ask, removing the oxygen mask so his glasses will fit down on his face. "Dad, you are dying. If you need it, I'm giving you permission to go." Taking hold of his hand, he quiets a little and looks at me. I know he is listening. "Do you remember my telling you and Mother about my experience of dying and going to the other side?"

"Oh yes, I remember," says my mother from the other side of the bed.

Dad nods his head.

"Remember, there is a light that you will need to follow," I say.

I spend some time helping dad to find the light. It is up and behind the forehead. His light is very dim, but I reassure him that the light will get brighter when he needs it.

"You are in for a great adventure, and you are well prepared," I say with reassurance.

Dad falls asleep and I leave. I have a long drive ahead.

*   *   *

"We talked about death and life, our life together. He was very relaxed," Mother relayed in a phone call the next day.

The following night Mother called me about 3:00 am.

"Your father has crossed over. Thanks for helping. He was at peace," Mother said through her tears.

LAST SAIL

We had been waiting a long time for a perfect day to sail. As usual, the summer winds in the San Francisco Bay area were strong and gusty.

I told my friend Tim that October will bring good sailing weather. Tim has a thirty-something racer-cruiser with wheel steering and a high aspect sail design. A design primarily for up wind sailing. After all, isn't that the way you win races? He wanted to experience small boat sailing. My physical condition of numbness and loss of strength in my hands and feet has kept me from sailing for over two years. I too was looking forward to sailing especially with somebody who could do all the work.

Last Saturday was the perfect day. My 15-foot sailboat *Test Bed* was ready to go. We launched at the Richmond Harbor ramp, about 10:30am, behind all the power boat fishermen eager to get out on the weekend. The tide was high, the ramp down to the dock was easy for my walker, and it was a beautiful day. I had mounted "grab poles" to help me get on and off the boat. Tim did all the work of rigging the standing lug sail. I could see he was impressed by the ease of rigging; the mast just dropped into place and was ready to go. The lug sail has only three lines: a halyard to raise the sail, a down haul attached the tack clew to tighten the leading edge of the sail, and a sheet to control the set of the sail.

I took the helm, Tim cast off, two quick tacks, a close miss of the end of the next pier, and on to open water. Only a sailor knows the joy of sailing again after a long hiatus. Tim adjusted the curve of the sail using the tension on the downhaul for close hauled or off wind tacks. I demonstrated how to change the rake of the mast by simply moving a wedge. Tim's grin confirmed his enjoyment of small boat sailing.

I passed the helm to Tim. It did not take long for him to learn the use of a tiller. He was impressed by the quick response of a center board boat. The wind was a perfect eight knots, gentle with no gusts, but strong enough to fill the sail and give us a noticeable wake. Tim experimented with how close the boat would point. On off-wind tacks, he was surprised at how fast the boat traveled. He admitted that his boat did not do as well off the wind.

This was a good day, a good sail, and Tim was a good sailor. I sat back, stretched out my legs, and let the memories and images begin to flow. Perhaps *Test Bed* was talking to me. Once, years ago, while sailing on a High Sierra lake, I had difficulty staying with the wind which kept changing direction. A few days later, hiking on the ridge above the lake, I looked down and saw the pattern of the wind on the lake's surface. The wind riffles looked like an asterisk printed on the water as the downward wind hit the lake and separated into many different directions.

Meeting the challenges of the wind as well as the complexities of waterways is one of the reasons I love to gunk hole. I have sailed alone, with my dog, and often with friends. Over the years I have sailed many of the backwaters in Northern California but sailing the tidal rivers has been the most enjoyable. The Napa River above the city is not considered navigable so there are no bridge clearance numbers posted. Once, sailing at about half tide, my mast was able to clear the 3rd Street Bridge and just cleared the 2nd Street Bridge. However, I knew I would have to drop my mast for the next bridge. I surprised a Green Heron fishing along the riverbank. They're about the size of a sea gull, but elusive and seldom seen. When it did see me, it quickly disappeared into the shore grasses.

I sailed on with the incoming tide until I bottomed out. The tide turned. Both the dog and I stepped out to relieve ourselves. I placed a stick in the mud at the edge of the water to check the movement of the tide. When I returned to the boat, I was surprised at how much and how quickly the water had dropped. Swiftly turning the boat around, a difficult job now that the boat was aground, I headed downriver.

The Green Heron has remained elusive to me.

Another gunk holing experience happened on the Estero Americano river which drains the vast ranch land of West Marin, north of San Francisco. With permission from the rancher to cross his land, I followed the creek in my pickup and boat trailer, towards the ocean until it was wide enough and deep enough to launch my boat. The rancher had never seen a sailboat on the Estero, only an occasional canoe or kayak. It was early morning, a light breeze followed the meandering course of the Estero through the hills. I had to start the outboard. If the wind picked up in the afternoon, it would be a great sail back. After a while I tired of the sound of the motor and ran the boat up on the bank. The hike to the top of the hill passed through a carpet of wildflowers. At the top, as far as the eye could see, were blue and yellow and red and white flowers. It had been a wet spring and the flowers responded. Below me, the Estero snaked west to the ocean.

The mouth of the Estero was almost blocked by sand, creating a small lake with sandy beaches. There was not a person in sight. Nor had there been for a long time. The heavy winter rains had washed out the foot path down to the beach from the headland trail. I was completely alone, another joy of gunk holing. The wind did pick up and the sail back was faster than traveling by outboard.

Of all my gunk holing experiences, my favorites were exploring the tidal rivers on the Mendocino Coast. For two summers in the 1980s I lived in Mendocino while teaching stone carving at the Mendocino Art Center. Of all the rivers, Big River was my favorite. There is a flat, hard sand beach just upriver from the ocean surf, it makes a good launching site. The beach is part of the remains of the old logging industry and sawmill. There are numerous pilings, and a huge rusting wrought iron chain used to anchor a log boom, or a ship, or who knows what.

The best way to experience the river is to start in the morning, catch the incoming tide, and sail with the onshore wind. The tide flows upriver for about eight miles. In some places the river widens out to flow through marshes along the edge. Then it narrows to where the tree branches almost touch across the water. In one of these narrow places is the remains of an old splash dam. These dams where used to raise the water level in the river so the harvested redwood logs could be floated downstream. In the summer, the dams were dynamited open to allow the collection of giant logs to roar down river, to be caught by a log boom at the sawmill. This, of course, was an ecological disaster. The rushing water and the logs tore out everything in their path. There has been no logging in this area since the early 1930s. It is good to see the river healing and returning to its pristine state.

After a few hours of sailing upriver, the lifting incoming tide is almost spent. The onshore wind is also softening. It was here in Mendocino that I added the tops'l to my rig to catch the winds higher up. The river flows out of a large meadow. The meadow was built up by the runoff from clear cutting the forests on the surrounding hills in the late 1800s. The river narrows, the boat brushes along the grass on both sides. This is as far upriver as I can travel.

The only way to return is to lift the bow up on the grass and swing the boat around. I remember to lift with my legs, not my back. In the water, I see a large fish continuing up stream. Maybe it is a salmon. I sit on the bow for a little rest. There are no man-made sounds, no roads, no power lines. Time stands still. Or better yet, time seems to stack up, layer upon layer. It's almost like stacks of movie film which had been recorded and shown, and are now waiting to be viewed again. One image is the time of the logging of the giant redwoods, wood to be used for building the ornate Victorian homes in San Francisco. Before the logging was the time of the Pomo who called this their land. Their homes were located far enough inland to be out of the coastal fog, enjoying the same sun that I too am feeling now.

And back and back in time until time seemed to circle around to the present. The fish have returned and now even the redwoods have regrown. Maybe not the giant first growth of before, but tall, hundred-year-old trees.

I become aware of a new sound, the trickle of water flowing. The tide has turned and I must finish lifting the boat around and head down river.

I wish that there was a better sounding name for this sailing experience than "gunk holing."

* * *

Tim was doing a great job of sailing. I set the memories aside. The afternoon winds were just picking up. It was time to head in. The day had given Tim many new experiences sailing a small boat. There was one more I would like to share with him. He was accustomed to having his sail's sheets cleated down. On a long tack the length of the harbor, I released the sail sheet from the jam cleat and placed the line in Tim's hand.

Keep one hand on the tiller,
and hold the sheet in the other hand.
Through the tiller and the rudder,
you have touched all the waters of the world.
By holding the sheet, and controlling the sail,
you have made contact with the currents
and the winds of the earth's air.
You are in control of these two great fluids of the earth.
You are the captain of your ship.
This is co-creating with the earth.
Feel the power between your hands,
between your arms, and across your chest.
Let this power flow through your heart,
and claim it as your own.

Already, as I write this, the memory of the rest of the day is fading. When Tim and I returned to the dock, as hard as I tried, I was unable to get out of the boat. I had very little control and strength in my legs. With the help of three fishermen, Tim was able to get me up on the dock to my walker.

Test Bed has been washed down and put away. Our 40 years of sailing together is over.

It was a perfect day for my last sail.

Photo by Roger Slagle

LETTING GO

When I moved to the Bay Area in 1963, I was a skier. The snow on Portland, Oregon's Mt. Hood was not the best for skiing, but it was an easy hour drive from the college campus to the slopes. I loved to ski, feeling the wind in my face, and the snow slipping rapidly below my feet. What I liked best was gliding through the mountains, seeing the valleys and other peaks in the distance. This was not an experience of the flat prairies of western Kansas.

I arrived in California with my skis strapped to the roof of my car, eagerly waiting for ski season.

Graduate work was much harder than college. I needed to do something with my hands.

The ceramic class at the junior college was full, but there was room for me in the sculpture department. I knew nothing about sculpture, having only seen large public art in Europe and ancient sculptures in the Louvre.

The instructor gave each of us a lump of clay and said to make something. I fashioned a standing figure about eight inches tall. It did not stand up. I did not know about using a wire armature to give the sculpture support. I stood the piece up, but again it fell.

I looked at this little collapsed figure, a pile of body parts. The head was thrown back, seeming to howl a primordial scream of despair. I was in awe. For the first time I had communicated non-verbally, expressing deep feelings which had been ignored up to now.

The instructor asked how long had I been sculpting.

"About 20 minutes," I said. "This is my first."

"Well," he said. "You've got something. Keep going."

By the time winter came I was intensely involved in my graduate studies, working a mundane job, sculpting steel in my girlfriend's carport, and casting bronze at the local junior college sculpture department. Although I longed to experience Lake Tahoe's perfect snow conditions, challenging slopes, and magnificent vistas, Lake Tahoe was a hard four-hour drive away, the lift tickets were expensive, and skiing often required an overnight stay. I could not afford skiing, or the risk of an injury. The decision not to go was eased by my new passion. I looked forward to weekends of sculpting time.

For 60 years, sculpting has been my passion. With the close collaboration of my inner creative self, I sculpted pieces expressing beauty and feelings which could not be expresses verbally. I moved from bronze casting to direct carving in marble because the material itself is a part of the message being conveyed. Marble is of the earth, bronze is man-made.

Letting go of experiencing the external beauty of skiing in the mountains made room for the inner beauty of my sculptures.

Selling my beloved sailboat in Seattle had also been difficult. The boat had been a meeting place, a time of father/son sharing. A connection so vital for a high school senior beginning his life's journey. But the selling of the boat was necessary for my transition to college. It did not, however, diminish the bond established and solidified between a father and a young adult son.

Often, when one door closes behind me, another opens to something better. I trust this. But sometimes, in the dark corridors of life, the door has slammed shut with a bang, and all the doors in the hallway are closed and locked. It's a challenge to know what to do.

There comes a time in life when letting go is a major factor in daily life. This is where I am now as I go into my 83rd year. I wish I could say it is an interesting process. What I can say is… it is in process.

I have written several articles on this topic: letting go of my sailing, letting go of holding tools, letting go of being able to walk without assistance, first a staff, then two walking sticks, and after a few falls, using a walker. First it was a two-wheel walker with tennis balls on the back of two legs. This walker did not work on anything but smooth surfaces. I investigated three-wheel and four-wheeled Rollator walkers. I experimented with six-inch and eight-inch plastic or rubber wheels, even converted one to twelve-inch wheels. All a part of the process.

My favorite sculptures, ones I had kept in my studio and enjoyed for many years, have all been donated to the educational nonprofit 1440 Multiversity for others to enjoy. After the installation, I thought I would return to visit my sculptures with friends. We could enjoy and share stories of each piece. But I have not been back even once. I have let go. The boats, which were such a big part of my life, have all been sold or given away. I miss sailing. Recently a friend took me out sailing on the Bay in his boat. I had not been sailing for over three years. It was a good sail. The best part was coming to the realization that I have let go of sailing.

With the condition of my physical body now, I'm ready to let go. But when?

I believe Ram Das when he said: "Death is the greatest adventure of all

        that's why it saved to last."

But when?

If my emotions hit depression, sadness, or anger at something in the present, I realize it is an indicator. It is a reminder that I'm out of sync with my inner self. I do not want to be critical of my emotions anymore than I would judge the indicator on my gas gauge when it shows the tank is only half full.

A few weeks ago, when feeling more sadness than usual, I asked for help during my meditation.

"Just observe, watch what is happening," said my inner guiding voice.

"Then I'll write about it," I replied.

"No," said my guidance. "It's not an assignment, just watch. It happens only once in a lifetime."

So, when my fingers can't hold a cup of coffee, I observe. My fingers do not work better, but I get less angry at the situation. This makes for a better day.

FLIGHT FEATHERS

Something is happening
    all too fast.
Yesterday, I lost a feather
    It was a flight feather
Today, I lost two more.
Yesterday, I tried to glue it back on
    It would not stick
Today, I tried to pick them up.
    They kept slipping out of my hands.

This is no mid-life molt.

Some day (or night)
    I will fly again. I'll not need feathers
With a hop, and a skip, and a grin on my face
    I'll speed to what Ram Das calls
The greatest adventure of all,
    that is why it is saved to last.

ACKNOWLEDGEMENTS

Everything is true. But not necessarily factual.

All of theses stories are true.

Some are even pure fact.

Others include beliefs, make believes, and even misbeliefs.

All are based on my personal experiences.

This collection was never intended to be exclusively a memoir or autobiographical.

These experiences were powerful enough to become embedded in my brain, many are 60 and even 75 years old.

My life has added some insights to the stories, making them more vivid.

Truth may include fact, but it can also include belief.

This book would never have been completed without my friend, mentor, teacher, and editor Tim Crandle. He read an early story of mine and encouraged me to write. My writing, thanks to Tim, has become the focus of my creativity.

ABOUT THE AUTHOR

Welton Rotz has been a sculptor of stone and metal, a blacksmith, licensed general contractor, boat builder and teacher. In the early 1960s he pursued graduate studies in Theology. Disenchanted with church doctrine, Welton did not complete his degree, preferring to seek his spirituality through meditation, extensive research, and his creativity. He went on to study psychotherapy.

Born in 1940, Welton lived with relatives on a wheat and cattle farm for six months before moving to the Philippines with his college professor parents at the age of nine. After four years overseas, Welton returned to the states. He spent every summer during high school and college farming with his uncle and cousin in western Kansas. Sculpting and sailing have been his passion for many years.

In 2015 Welton was diagnosed with a rare, progressive amyloid neurological disease which severely impacted his hands and feet.

He lives in San Francisco with his wife Barbara Stuart and an Icelandic sheepdog named Mikilee. There, he types stories with a stick held between his bent fingers.

www.ingramcontent.com/pod-product-compliance
Lightning Source LLC
Chambersburg PA
CBHW060548260626
47161CB00003B/1101